Dear Romance Reader,

Welcome to a world of breathtaking passion and never-ending romance.
Welcome to *Precious Gem Romances*.

It is our pleasure to present *Precious Gem Romances*, a wonderful new line of romance books by some of America's best-loved authors. Let these thrilling historical and contemporary romances sweep you away to far-off times and places in stories that will dazzle your senses and melt your heart.

Sparkling with joy, laughter, and love, each *Precious Gem Romance* glows with all the passion and excitement you expect from the very best in romance. Offered at a great affordable price, these books are an irresistible value—and an essential addition to your romance collection. Tender love stories you will want to read again and again, *Precious Gem Romances* are books you will treasure forever.

Look for eight fabulous new *Precious Gem Romances* each month—available only at Wal★Mart.

Lynn Brown, Publisher

TOYS AND WISHES

Karen Rose Smith

Nancy, Christmas in June! I hope you enjoy it All my best. Karen Rose Smith

Zebra Books
Kensington Publishing Corp.

http://www.zebrabooks.com

ZEBRA BOOKS are published by

Kensington Publishing Corp.
850 Third Avenue
New York, NY 10022

First Printing: December, 1996
10   9   8   7   6   5   4   3   2   1

Printed in the United States of America

In memory of my Aunt Helen.
Love, Karen

Chapter One

"What in blazes is going on here?"

Lexa Kittredge almost dropped the porcelain figurine she'd lifted from Clare Flannigan's bookshelf. Before she could answer, Clare slipped from behind the desk she'd been dusting.

"Josh! You're back!" She pushed her blue glasses farther up her nose. "Lexa, this is my nephew, Josh Flannigan. Josh, meet Alexandra Kittredge."

Lexa only had time to nod before Clare rushed on, "So how was Colorado, Josh? You deserved that long vacation. Anything exciting happen? Meet any bears?"

Lexa suppressed a smile, recognizing Clare's attempt to turn the focus of the conversation on her nephew, rather than the disordered state of her apartment.

"Aunt Clare, what's going on?"

His question was directed at Clare but his gaze was on Lexa. Suddenly she wished they'd opened a window. She hadn't noticed it before, but the heat in Clare's apartment was stifling. Her sweatshirt was sticking uncomfortably to her shoulders. It wasn't supposed to be this hot in Pennsylvania in October, Indian summer or not. Or did the sudden rise in temperature have something to do with Josh

Flannigan's piercing blue eyes, the same startling blue as Clare's?

"I'm moving."

Josh's attention flew to his aunt. "You're what?"

Clare climbed onto the step stool to remove books from the top shelf of the bookcase. "I'm moving. Some friends and I have invested in a lovely old house," she explained airily as if she did something like this at least once a week.

Josh's fingers dashed through his shaggy black hair. "Have you taken leave of your senses?"

Lexa set the figurine back on the shelf and took a step forward, deciding it might be time to help Clare explain the situation to her nephew. She offered her hand. "It's a pleasure to meet you, Mr. Flannigan. Clare's told me so much about you."

Josh's gaze switched back to her. "And just who are you?"

"Joshua, don't be rude!" Clare scolded.

He took Lexa's hand but also took the time to give her a more thorough looking-over. She didn't have to guess at what he saw. Sweatshirt and jeans. Curly blond hair that probably looked as if she'd just escaped a stiff wind. Shiny face. "I'm a friend of Clare's."

He dropped her hand. "Since when?"

"Josh . . . "

"It's all right, Clare. About two months ago Clare came to a workshop I was giving," Lexa explained.

"About?" Josh looked at Clare as if she'd been bitten by some strange bug.

"Senior citizens developing second careers."

"Oh, great. Just what Clare needs when she's finally retired."

"You don't know what I need." Clare's tone matched the fiery hue of her red hair.

"Mr. Flannigan, your aunt has acted very responsibly."

"Where did you get the money?" Josh asked his aunt.

"I had money saved."

Josh's hand slashed through the air. "But that was your nest egg. I don't believe you've done something so . . . impulsive."

Lexa took a deep breath. She had to do something to prevent a full-blown fight. "I've directed Clare to an experienced financial advisor."

Josh shook his head and rubbed the back of his neck. "Clare, you can't be serious about moving. You've lived in this apartment all your life. I've lived here much of mine. The rent's always been reasonable, you don't have to worry about mowing grass or shoveling snow." He looked around the room at the chaos. "My God! I go away for six weeks, and when I come back, you're packing boxes."

Clare shrugged and took Lexa's place at the bookshelves. She reached to the top shelf for two volumes of poetry. "I'm doing the right thing. Ask Lexa."

Lexa's voice was quiet. "I think you're doing what you want to do. That makes it right."

Striding toward Clare, Josh took the books from her hand and dumped them into an open carton. His denim jacket emphasized the width of his shoulders, and his snug-fitting jeans encased long legs and muscular thighs. He wasn't drop-dead handsome, but even with the beard stubble, he'd certainly do. Do for what? Lexa asked herself, then pushed every possible answer out of her head.

"I want to know where you got this crazy idea," Josh was saying. "Do you know the work you're letting yourself in for? The hassles?"

Clare's eyes threw rebellious darts. "What about the joy? The challenge? The thrill of a new adventure? Just because I'm over sixty, Joshua Flannigan, is no reason to put me out to pasture. I'm still alive and kicking more than ever. Thirty-five years of teaching English to teenagers is not enough to put me in a rocking chair."

She pointed her finger at him. "*You* thought I'd be happy retired. Well, if it wasn't for the senior center this past year, I'd have gone crazy! I expected more support from you."

Josh pushed his jacket flaps aside and stuffed his hands in his back pockets as if he were considering the best way to reason with his aunt. "Don't you think you're acting recklessly?"

Lexa squared her shoulders. This was going to be more

difficult than she'd expected. "Mr. Flannigan, your aunt came to talk to me because she was bored, because she was feeling useless, because sitting here by herself was making her feel ancient."

Josh's blue eyes were steady and concerned as they swung back to Clare. "Aunt Clare, all you have to do is call me. I can spend more time with you."

"What nonsense!" Clare planted her hands on her hips. "You're thirty-four. You have your own life to live and so do I."

Realizing her presence increased the tension, Lexa stepped forward. "Clare, it might be better if I wait in the other room."

"Don't let Josh chase you out."

Lexa crossed the room. "He's not. I think you two need to hash this out on your own. I'll take down the wall decorations in the living room."

Josh moved aside to let Lexa pass, wondering how to keep his aunt from making the biggest mistake of her life. He cared about her too much to let her put herself in financial jeopardy, let alone create more work for herself than she needed.

Lexa's delicate perfume lingered, teasing him. After weeks of smelling only damp earth and woods, the scent affected him. Or maybe it was her seeming fragility—the big brown eyes, that fluffy blond hair. She certainly looked harmless. So what was she doing meddling in Clare's life?

Josh turned toward his aunt, his black brows pulling together in an effort to concentrate on her problem. "A rambling old house is a real headache. Think of the money you'll waste on repairs. Something always needs to be fixed in old houses. Who's going to pay for that?"

Clare's tone was defensive. "Lexa says it doesn't need many repairs. The door frames need a fresh coat of paint. That's all."

The last thing he wanted to do was dismiss or hurt Clare's feelings. She had given him a home since he was twelve, and he loved her dearly. But the idea of her giving up her nest egg worried him. If Alexandra Kittredge had influenced Clare unduly, there'd be hell to pay.

"How does Lexa know what repairs this house needs?" Josh asked, amazed at the confidence Clare was placing in a stranger who could be a con artist. Not that she looked like one.

"She knows the real estate agent. She says he's honest and would tell us if anything else was wrong. My partners and I looked at the whole place carefully."

Partners. His aunt was in over her head; he knew it. "You have no experience dealing with people who might be less than honest. A real estate agent has one thing on his mind—selling. As for your partners, who are they and what do they know?"

Clare's lips tightened. "I do not have the time or inclination to keep arguing with you. I have to be packed in five days."

"Five days? You mean the deal's closed? You did this without consulting me?"

His aunt struggled to keep her voice even. "I'm an adult. I don't have to consult you. And how could I anyway when you were off backpacking in the woods?"

"You could have waited. You knew my timetable."

She gently clasped his arm. "I'm doing this whether you approve or not. We had to move fast on the house. Someone else wanted it. We settle on Friday and I intend to move in Saturday."

Whenever he argued with Clare, he felt as if he were running against the wind. He wanted what was best for her but he wasn't sure this was it. "You're moving too fast; I don't like the whole thing."

His aunt gave him a pat, then crossed to the desk and picked up a can of furniture polish. "I've made my decision, Josh. You're not going to change my mind so you might as well stop trying. I have a lot to do and not much time to do it. If you're going to help, you're welcome to stay."

Josh closed his eyes for a moment. He was tired. He had driven the last seven hours, anxious to get home, anxious to see how the toy stores were faring without him, anxious to find out what his aunt had been up to. He'd never expected this.

"I'm going to talk to Ms. Kittredge."

"You're not going to bully her. This was my decision."

"I want to know some details."

"So ask me!"

"You're too busy packing."

"Josh—"

"Aunt Clare," he parroted with the same wary intonation.

Clare threw her hands up in surrender. "Okay. But don't make her feel guilty. She's been an extraordinary help. I wouldn't have been able to do this without her."

Josh believed that. But why had she torn his aunt's life apart? He was determined to find out exactly what Lexa Kittredge had to do with this whole mess, and what kind of influence she obviously held over his aunt.

His footsteps were muffled by the carpet in the hallway. But when he entered the living room, Lexa turned toward him, as if sensing he was there.

She propped the painting she was holding against a sofa arm and sat down next to it. "Clare is sure about the plans she's made."

Josh's expression was grim. "Are they her plans or someone else's?"

Lexa stared up at him and didn't seem to take offense at his protective concern. "They're *her* plans."

There were smudges of blue under Lexa's eyes. Did she stay up late? Did she live with someone? He glanced at her hand. No ring on her finger. He wondered how she spent her free time and whom she spent it with, then immediately banished the thought.

He had to remind himself she could be manipulating his aunt for some gain of her own. His words were brisk. "Convince me. Convince me that you had nothing to do with her pouring her life savings into an old house, nothing to do with her turning her life topsy-turvy at her age. She said you've been advising her. What gives you that right?"

"I have that right because I have the qualifications and because I'm her friend. I have been since the workshop."

He crossed his arms over his chest. "I can't believe she

was interested in a second career. She can't possibly want to work again. She has a good teacher's pension."

"Why wouldn't she want to work again?" Lexa sat farther back on the sofa, clearly making herself at home.

"She doesn't need to. Her pension is healthy and she's financially secure."

Lexa shook her head. "Maybe she doesn't need to work for material reasons, but she needs—"

"How do *you* know what she needs? You can't just advise people without knowing their situation."

Her cheeks flushed. "Mr. Flannigan, I majored in social work and I minored in psychology. I run a job counseling and placement center. I didn't go looking for your aunt, she approached me. She was sad, depressed."

Josh felt as if she'd kicked him in the stomach. "Depressed? She's always smiling, whistling, doing something. Clare's *never* depressed. She's the happiest person I know."

"Relatives always seem to be the last to see discontent. If you had really listened to Clare, you might have realized . . . " When he was about to interrupt, Lexa held up her hand like a stop sign. "Please let me finish."

He stuffed his hands in his pockets and gave her a nod to go ahead.

"Clare's friends at the center know she's been unhappy the past year. They persuaded her to come to the workshop and to see me. After we talked, I realized she didn't really want to get back in the work force, but she wanted something to put meaning in her life."

"So you advised a venture that could wipe out her life savings and give her more work than she can handle."

"I advised no such thing. I told her to think about what she liked to do, what she wanted to do, and what she did best. *She* took it from there. She talked to other seniors and discovered she wasn't the only one who was feeling lonely and empty. She wants to care for people. That's what she did for thirty-five years. She found two other people who want to do the same thing. They want to share their lives, take care of and depend on each other."

Josh was feeling more and more uncomfortable. "And

I suppose you don't get anything out of this? You're just a do-gooder who goes around solving people's problems?"

Lexa's eyes told him that she had heard the accusation before. "I've helped Clare find a road that will bring her happiness. You're not thinking about her life. You're thinking about the easiest route for yourself so you don't have to worry about her."

The static between them crackled. "You have no right to judge me."

She stood. "And you have no right to judge my motives or your aunt's capabilities. Clare has wisdom, experience, maturity, and goals. She's smart, interesting, and has a lot to share and no one to share it with."

"She has me!"

Lexa tipped her head back. "And you think you're enough to fill her world? Get serious. That might have been true when you were a recalcitrant teenager, but it's certainly not true now."

He felt at a definite disadvantage. If his aunt had told this woman about some of his escapades, Lexa was one up on him.

"You have an answer for everything, don't you?" he goaded, suddenly wanting to get a rise out of her. He stepped closer. Lexa's perfume wafted around his head; his heart suddenly beat harder. A surge of desire startled him.

"No, I don't. But I've had experience with scores of people."

"The truth is you feel powerful influencing people's lives, changing their direction," he accused.

"The truth is, Mr. Flannigan, it makes me feel good, not powerful. The truth is you don't want your aunt to be independent and not need you. Actually I don't think you'd know the truth if it bit you in the seat of your too-tight jeans!"

Josh tried to regroup. "I want what's best for Clare, what's good for her."

"You might not know what that is. Only she knows. I'll leave so you can discuss this without interference."

He reached for Lexa's arm, and when his fingers closed

around it, he saw the same jolt of awareness he experienced reflected in her eyes. "Don't leave without saying goodbye to her. She'll think I ran you out the door."

"Clare loves you. She needs and wants your support. This isn't easy for her."

Josh's eyes narrowed. Lexa sounded so sincere. He released her arm and let his hand drop to his side. "I want to see her happy. But I want her safe."

"Even people over sixty might have to take risks to find happiness."

Had Lexa Kittredge taken many risks in her life? He decided to find out more about her. But not now. His aunt was his primary concern. He didn't stand in Lexa's way when she started toward the den to tell Clare she was leaving. He watched the sway of her hips as she walked, and he made up his mind. No, he and Alexandra Kittredge weren't finished yet. Not by a long shot.

After Lexa returned to her town house from Clare's apartment Sunday evening, she showered and made herself a salad. Wrapped in a chenille robe, she settled on the sofa. Momentary thoughts of Josh Flannigan teased at her, but she put them out of her consciousness. She had much more on her mind than a meaningless attraction to a handsome man.

The phone rang and interrupted her reverie. She heard her sister Dani's voice on the answering machine and grabbed the phone on the end table.

"Dani, I'm here." Lexa flicked off the tape recording. "How are you feeling?"

"About the same. The doctor says the nausea will pass in a couple of months. I saw a lawyer."

"And?"

"He doesn't feel there will be any problems as long as we're both sure this is what we want. He said to think about it for another month or so then call him and he'll start the paperwork. Lexa, are you sure you want to adopt? It's too hard to raise a child as a single parent. That's why I . . . "

Lexa's heart tore as she heard Dani's anguish. At that moment she despised the man who refused to support Dani. "Honey, it's different for me. I have a sound income. I have access to good day care here in Chambersburg. You know, *you* could do it if you really want to. Dad would help you."

Tears threaded Dani's voice. "I can't do it, Lexa. You're strong. I can't believe how you've done everything on your own without Daddy's money."

"That was my choice. But you can accept his help."

"I don't want to raise a child alone. And I can't believe you do."

Lexa had loved and protected Dani since their mother died. "Did you tell Dad yet?"

"No. Not yet. And don't you."

"I won't. But you should tell him soon."

"I will. Eventually. He'll think I should get married to save the family name or something. What a laugh. Marriage is the last thing Rob wants to think about."

"Have you seen him lately?"

"Yes. We argued again. Lexa, I love him but he doesn't want to get married. I told him you're going to adopt the baby. He thinks you're crazy."

Lexa knew exactly what she was doing. Crazy didn't enter into it. A severe case of endometriosis had affected her chances of bearing children, and the knowledge had plagued her for the last two years. No one knew but Dani. When she had learned that her sister was pregnant but wanted to give the baby up for adoption, Lexa had jumped at the chance. "I can't tell you how thankful I am you're willing to let me adopt."

"You've always been a terrific big sister. And I know you'll make a great mother because you care so much about everyone."

"Hey, you better stop before I get a swelled head." The teasing tone disappeared. "I only want you to do what's right for you. I want you to be happy. Okay?"

Dani's sigh came through loud and clear. "Okay." After a pause, she asked, "What time do you think you can be here Saturday?"

"About eleven-thirty? Twelve?"

"The earlier the better. You're the only one I can talk to right now."

Dani expected Lexa to be around whenever she needed her, and Lexa always was. "I'll get there as soon as I can. Take care. Okay?"

"Will do. See you Saturday."

Lexa put down the receiver, wishing she could protect her sister better . . . more. Not unlike the way Josh wanted to protect his aunt. But Clare was mature. Sixty-three years old. Dani was immature, sometimes irrepressible, and rebellious even at twenty-one.

Lexa's thoughts returned to Josh. The brilliance of his blue eyes and the strength of his chin remained vivid in her mind. If things were different, she might want to get to know him better. But getting involved with a man now was out of the question.

Chapter Two

Monday afternoon, Lexa pulled open the glass door and stepped into The Toy Tank—Josh Flannigan's store. Looking around at the neat, organized displays, she had a hard time connecting the shaggy, beard-stubbled backpacker she'd met with the owner of this successful toy store.

Clare had told her how Josh had majored in business management in college, worked six years for a retail chain, saving every penny he could, and at twenty-eight had put a down payment on this building and opened The Toy Tank. Now he had two stores—one in Chambersburg, one in Harrisburg.

Passing down an aisle stacked high with Halloween costumes, Lexa smiled. At the service desk she asked for Mr. Flannigan and the employee pointed to an office at the rear of the store.

Lexa walked toward it, feeling as if she were confronting the lion in his den. She'd thought a lot about Clare and her nephew and didn't want to come between them.

True, he'd always been an integral part of Clare's life, but Clare's life was changing. If only he could accept it . . .

Lexa stopped short when she saw him through the glass window. What a transformation! His hair was trimmed, but its thick waves defied attempts to be styled. His face was clean-shaven. Sexy in jeans, he was even sexier in his navy pinstripe suit. His blue shirt made his eyes a deeper blue when he looked up and saw her.

The suspicion was still there.

The door to his office stood open. She stepped inside. "Hi. Do you have a few minutes?"

His expression was guarded. "Sure. Have a seat."

He perched on the corner of the desk while she sat in the leather chair in the corner.

"Clare called me this morning."

He sighed. "To ask you to talk to me."

"Yes, but I told her this was between the two of you." Josh's brows lifted.

"I don't want to come between you."

"But you are. Your name crops up every two sentences." Lexa shifted uneasily in her chair. "We've become friends."

"Why?"

"Because ... " She couldn't tell him she looked on Clare as the mother she'd lost. Her stepmother had been a poor substitute. "We clicked the moment we met."

Josh stood and went behind his desk. "I apologize for my attitude yesterday. I'd driven all day and was looking forward to taking Clare to dinner. When I found chaos instead ... " He shrugged and smiled.

It was a disarming smile. She'd known many men who didn't know how to apologize. She relaxed and smiled back. "I'm afraid I didn't help much. I'm sorry I ... blew up."

"Maybe I needed to hear what you had to say. I really do have her best interests at heart."

Lexa sat forward, feeling she was making progress. "I know. She's told me you're more of a son than a nephew."

He pulled out the swivel chair and sat behind his desk. "And what else did she tell you?"

An imp made Lexa say, "Something about catching you skinny-dipping with your girlfriend after your high school graduation party. How difficult it was to teach you how to drive under the speed limit. How you traded two of her oldest silver dollars for a frog . . . ''

"Stop. Stop!" he pleaded. "Or you'll have me blushing before your eyes."

"As if anything could make you blush."

"I could think of a few things," he teased.

That winsome smile of his could melt Antarctica. The character lines that crinkled around his eyes when he smiled added to his charm. "Clare said you and she had reached an understanding."

He cocked his head. "We understand each other perfectly. She told me what she's planning to do and I gave my unnecessary stamp of approval because she would have done it anyway. If you hadn't noticed, she's a very stubborn woman."

"I wonder if it runs in the family."

He grinned. "You've noticed."

No man's smile had ever made her feel so . . . unsettled. She straightened and got to the point of her visit. "There's a meeting tonight at the senior center. I thought you might want to come and see what goes on. I'm sure Clare would like you to meet her friends, too."

Josh looked at Lexa strangely, as if he couldn't figure her out. "What time?"

"Seven."

"I'll be there."

His blue gaze was too penetrating. And she had more work back at her office than she wanted to think about. She stood. "Good. I'll see you there."

Josh nodded.

After Lexa left his office, Josh leaned back in his chair and propped his feet on the desk. He hadn't gotten much sleep last night, worrying about Clare, wondering what to do about Ms. Kittredge's influence. She seemed so damned honest . . . sincere. He glanced toward the store and saw the top of her curly blond head as she passed down the aisle.

He'd spoken to his lawyer that morning. And the real estate agent. Clare would lose money if she dropped out of the sale. Josh intended to inspect the property himself after work with a contractor he knew to see if the investment was sound.

And as for Alexandra Kittredge, there was only one way to find out her motives. He'd go to that meeting tonight and he'd get to know her better. If she was sincere and if she truly was Clare's friend, he wanted to find out how much influence she had over his aunt and whether it was good or bad. He'd neglected his aunt too much in the past year. That was going to stop.

He owed his aunt. Without Clare, he would have ended up in a boys' home or on the streets. Yep. He owed her big and he'd protect her whether she liked it or not. Whether Alexandra Kittredge liked it or not.

Lexa opened her hatchback as Josh walked toward her in the parking lot of the senior center. He must have been watching for her.

"Clare told me you'd have cartons to carry in." He reached into her trunk and stacked one box on top of another so he could carry both.

"Thank you." She shut the trunk.

As they walked toward the building, he asked, "What's in these?"

"Halloween costumes."

"What have you got?"

"The usual. Clowns, gypsies. What's your favorite?"

"Dracula," he drawled with an accent straight from Transylvania.

She laughed and opened the door for him.

Once inside the one-story building, Josh followed Lexa so he could observe her. The coat she wore was beige cashmere and she wore it as if she was used to quality. She greeted the groups scattered here and there who were talking and sipping coffee or punch. Everyone seemed to know her well.

From across the room, a bald man called, "Got a gorilla suit? I want hair for one night!"

Lexa called back, "We love you the way you are, Joe."

One of the ladies nudged Lexa's arm and whispered, "Isn't Clare's nephew cute?"

"Cute?" Josh mouthed at Lexa as he deposited the boxes on a cafeteria-style table.

She laughed. "Does that offend your macho sensibilities?"

"I much prefer hot, sexy—"

"Humble?"

"Once every decade or so," he acknowledged, his smile reaching his eyes.

A wiry-haired woman at the front of the room banged a gavel on the podium and asked, "Can everyone please be seated? We have a lot of ground to cover tonight."

Sitting in one of the back rows, Clare waved to Lexa and Josh. She squeezed Lexa's hand as she sat down and whispered, "He came!"

On Lexa's other side, Josh didn't seem to hear. Before Lexa could answer Clare, the woman up front said, "There's someone I'd like you all to meet. He's new to Chambersburg and I think he could be of help to many of us. He's a financial advisor. I'd like to introduce Mr. Stanley."

Lexa whispered to Clare, "We'll talk later."

A man in his late forties or early fifties stood and walked to the podium from the first row. "Thank you, Edna. How do you do, everyone? My name's Ted Stanley. When Edna came to see me, I told her what I could do for her. When she mentioned the senior center, I asked her if I could talk to all of you. I'll begin by saying that the elderly in this country are outliving their incomes. Social security isn't enough. Over half of the elderly have no private pensions—that's particularly true of widows."

Lexa saw many heads nod up and down.

"Is he the one you sent Clare to?" Josh asked, watching Lexa as she listened to the speaker.

"No, I sent her to a woman I knew was reputable."

That note of sincerity again. Were his doubts uncalled for?

As Stanley droned on about turning around negative credit ratings, getting loans even over age sixty, generalities about investments that could provide steady interest payments, Lexa took out a pencil and paper and made some notes.

Josh elbowed her arm. "Thinking of investing?"

"No. I want to check out his credentials. I don't like the idea he's targeting senior citizens." She seemed genuinely worried.

"What's unusual about that?"

"Retired people usually have their finances well in hand. They aren't a good market for a financial advisor. Unless he wants to do more than help. Unless he's unscrupulous." Almost to herself, she murmured, "I don't like his eyes."

Josh leaned close and whispered in her ear, "Any reason in particular?" Her scent wound around him and he enjoyed the closeness for a moment.

"No. It's just a feeling."

"Do you always judge people by their eyes?"

She stared straight ahead. "Most of the time."

"What do you think about *my* eyes?"

She turned her face to his to see if he was serious. Her lips were a half inch away from his. She cleared her throat and jerked her head back.

Josh whispered again, "Well?"

"I like your eyes," she admitted hoarsely.

He felt the same awareness that had made her voice husky. And reminded himself, *No way, Flannigan. She's a career woman through and through.* He'd done some checking. Lexa *was* involved with the senior center; she'd been instrumental in getting it started.

She'd established her job counseling service six years ago. According to Clare, she was also involved in Project Literacy and the YMCA. He didn't know how Lexa found time to brush her teeth. He'd been involved with a woman a few years ago who couldn't make time to have dinner let alone a relationship. Josh knew exactly what he wanted—a woman who knew how to play and did so on a regular basis.

A person needed time to play. He bet time was a precious commodity to Alexandra Kittredge and he still wondered why she'd make time for his aunt.

Stanley ended his spiel with, "I will be glad to see any of you who want to talk to me. Just call my office."

Lexa tried not to be so aware of Josh. But it wasn't easy. His cologne reminded her he was there, as did the pressure of his elbow against hers. She looked straight ahead.

Edna thanked the financial advisor for coming and turned to the rest of the agenda. "Lexa brought costumes for anyone who might need one for our Halloween Party on October thirtieth. Now I need a list of people to bring refreshments. Who's first?"

Edna formulated a list ranging from hot hors d'oeuvres to brownies. The group discussed plans to visit nursing homes with favors for Thanksgiving and Christmas, dates for social events in November, and the agenda for their next meeting. After Edna had taken notes, she asked, "Is there anything else we need to discuss?"

A woman in the third row raised her hand and stood. "I heard about a program in Carlisle. The senior citizens offer time to answer phones acting like Mr. and Mrs. Santa Claus. The numbers are published in the paper and on the news, and children can call during certain hours. Is anybody interested?" Several people raised their hands and she said, "See me after the meeting and we'll talk about it some more."

Lexa raised her hand, was recognized, and stood. "I want you to know the malls are hiring extra security guards for Christmas. So if any of you are interested in temporary work, let me know."

"Are they hiring women?" a woman with a blond rinse asked from the far right.

"If you can do the job, I don't see why not," Lexa answered with a smile. "You can always threaten to sue for discrimination if you have the qualifications and they won't interview you."

"Is there anything women don't want to do?" a gruff old gent who had served in the military for forty years grumbled.

He was answered by a lady three seats down the row. "Yeah, mister. Dishes. I've had enough for a lifetime."

Everyone who heard the exchange laughed. Lexa

grinned and said, "I do have openings strictly for men. Some of the stores need Santa Clauses."

Josh's baritone rang out. "Mine included."

Lexa looked at him with surprise. He shrugged and stood up. "My name's Josh Flannigan. Many of you might know my aunt Clare." Several heads bobbed. "I own The Toy Tank and I do need a Santa Claus. So if anyone's interested, see me after the meeting."

"Hey, maybe you could help us out," a man in the row in front of Josh commented. "Got any broken toys? We're fixin' 'em up for Toys for Tots to give to kids who won't get any."

"I sure do. They pile up until inventory when I get rid of them. If you think you can fix them, they're yours."

"We can fix 'em," came from several places in the crowd.

"I'll have my stock boy bring them over. Just let me know when you want them."

Lexa sat back down and so did Josh. She leaned toward him. "You sure know how to make friends and influence people."

"It comes with age."

"It comes with wanting to get involved. Look at Clare."

She was beaming as she gazed at her nephew.

Lexa could have sworn Josh's cheeks flushed.

After all the business was discussed and comments noted, the group was invited to socialize and snack on homemade cookies. A man approached Josh about being the store's Santa Claus.

Josh still managed to keep an eye on Lexa as she spoke with Clare. They mingled separately after that. He tried to discover what he could about this side of his aunt's life. He couldn't believe he'd gotten so out of touch. Business was one thing, enjoying himself on weekends at the shore or campgrounds was important too. But his aunt . . . she deserved more of his time than quick phone calls.

Josh looked around to find Lexa sitting at a table with an elderly man who was smoking a pipe. Her face was concerned, her pose attentive. She patted the man's hand and let hers rest on his.

Josh moved closer.

He heard her say, "I'm sorry, Milt. I hoped for your sake it would work out."

"There's no fool like an old fool," he quoted disparagingly. "Why did I ever think a woman thirty years younger than me would want me? Me, Milton Finch. She didn't want me. She only said she'd marry me so I'd keep buying her presents."

"Now, you don't know that," Lexa consoled.

"Yes, I do. She sure didn't give back the diamond bracelet or the fur coat or the Gucci pocketbook."

"Milt, did you have fun when she was with you?"

"Havin' that pretty young thing on my arm made me feel like a kid."

"Then it wasn't all bad, was it?"

He thought for a while. "No, I guess not. I sure felt great for a few months. But now, I feel so alone again."

"But nights like this help, don't they?"

"Yeah. I guess."

"You know, there are many attractive women around who are closer to your age."

"I suppose I haven't been lookin' at the right women. When I met Sandy at the grocery store and she seemed to like me, I thought it was meant to be."

"We all make mistakes."

"Yeah, but I'm not going to make the same one again. I'm going to look for a nice, down to earth, sixty-year-old woman."

"You might find her right here. Mrs. Grayson was terribly disappointed when you didn't come around for a few months."

"Flo Grayson, huh? She's pretty good lookin'."

Realizing the serious part of their conversation was over, Josh stepped closer to the table. Seeing him, Lexa stood. So did Milt. She introduced Milt to Josh.

After a handshake, Milt said, "I'm goin' to go get me some of them chocolate chip cookies. Lexa, I'll see you around. Josh, don't be a stranger. You play poker?"

"Now and then."

"Some afternoon you got free, you come join us."

Josh smiled as Milt ambled to the snack table.

"Have you met Clare's housemates?" Lexa asked.

"Yes, I have. In fact, the three of them are going back to Clare's apartment to discuss decorating plans."

Lexa smiled at Josh's expression. "That's not one of your interests?"

He grinned. "Wallpaper patterns don't turn me on." Lexa's wide eyes seemed to ask him what did. A devil inside him said, *You*. He grimaced inwardly. At least he hadn't said it out loud.

Alexandra Kittredge intrigued him and he still wasn't sure why she devoted so much time to helping others. "While Clare and her friends plan, would you like to have a drink with me? There's a quiet pub down the street."

"Oh, I don't know. I have mounds of paperwork at home—"

"One drink? I'm sure Clare would like us to get to know each other better."

Lexa glanced at his aunt happily chattering with Edna. "All right. Maybe a cup of coffee."

If Lexa was as friendly as she seemed to be and willing to talk to him, what could she have to hide? His heart felt lighter.

Josh took Lexa's coat from the table and held it for her. As she slipped her arms into the sleeves, his thumbs brushed her neck. He felt her start in response. So soft. So touchable. Her eyes met his. There were golden sparks in her gaze that said passion lurked not far below the surface. The thought excited him.

He reached out and straightened her lapel. When she wore high heels, her eyes were almost the same level as his.

He smiled and motioned toward the door. "Shall we go?"

After their goodbyes to Clare and her friends, they walked the short block to the pub. The fall breeze tossed Lexa's curls. The streetlight flickered through them, making the blondest strands glow.

Her high heels clicked on the pavement.

"Have you lived in Chambersburg all your life?" he asked casually, needing to start somewhere.

"No. I came here with a friend one year on spring break. I liked its size and the people."

"How did you know your business would work here?"

"Research. I put surveys in restaurants and at the YMCA. I talked to local business owners."

She was thorough and inventive. "Starting a business isn't easy."

She stuffed her hands in her pockets. The night air was getting colder. "I know. Especially when the only credit rating I had was my good standing on my car loan."

"You couldn't get help from your family?"

"I didn't *want* help from my family."

"You have problems with them?"

She glanced at him. "Doesn't everybody?"

"That's a side step if I ever heard one."

She met his gaze for a moment. "My father and I don't see eye to eye."

"And your mom?"

"She died when I was ten."

They had something in common. "I'm sorry. That's a rough break for a child."

"Clare told me you lost both your parents."

"When I was twelve. Thank God I had Clare."

"She means a lot to you."

"More than I can say."

When they reached the pub, Josh opened the heavy steel door and let Lexa precede him inside. He waited until his eyes adjusted to the dim lighting, then found them a table in the back. There were a few patrons sitting at the bar, but only two of the ten barrel-like tables were occupied.

After Josh hung Lexa's coat on the rack, he pulled out her chair. She looked surprised as she sat and murmured, "Thank you."

He picked up the menus and handed her one. "Their sandwiches are good."

"A cup of coffee will be fine."

The lights from the globed candle on the table glimmered in her eyes. "I didn't take time for supper. Did you?"

She shrugged. "Yogurt."

He couldn't prevent his gaze from lingering on her rose sweater dress. It showed every curve to perfection. He smiled. "Hasn't Clare lectured you about eating balanced meals?"

She laughed. "All the time. You, too?"

"All the time."

The waitress approached and asked for their order.

Lexa decided on a bowl of corn chowder and a cup of coffee. Josh ordered the roast beef club.

He enjoyed Lexa's company, but he wasn't here for that. He was here to find out more about her. "You really care about the people you work with, don't you?"

"I enjoy what I do. I like helping people."

"It's more than that. I was listening when you were talking to Milt."

She shrugged. "There are so many people, especially older people, who don't have anyone to listen to them. It only takes a few minutes and it makes them feel better."

He wanted to know what made her so fiercely compassionate. "And who listens to you?"

"What?"

"Everybody needs somebody. Who do you talk to?"

"Lots of people."

Josh gave her a considering look, not believing her. It seemed to him she was fairly independent. If she wouldn't even take help from her family to start her business . . .

The waitress brought their food. Josh's sandwich was enormous, at least two inches thick. Potato chips were piled high in the middle.

He offered her a wedge. "Go ahead. I don't want my jeans to get any tighter."

The amusement in his voice brought a pink blush to her cheeks. "I'm sorry about some of the things I said."

"Which ones?"

"About you thinking only of yourself. I don't know you well enough to judge. Your relationship with Clare is your business."

"But you'd fight like a tigress to see her happy. Why?" The question he'd been wanting to ask. Yet it came out differently than he'd expected.

"Clare's the type of person I'd imagine my mother to be if she'd lived."

What the hell could he say to that? Could he doubt the brightness of Lexa's eyes, the sincerity in her voice? What could she possibly have to gain by befriending his aunt?

Lexa ate the wedge of sandwich. She couldn't believe she'd said that. She never disclosed personal information indiscriminately. But something about the directness of Josh's blue eyes had gotten through her defenses. She looked down at her pink-tipped nails.

She had seen male interest off and on in his gaze tonight. She wasn't immune. When he'd helped her with her coat and his fingers brushed her neck, the ripple of electricity had sent heat from her head to her toes.

But none of that mattered. Her life was in transition. She couldn't get involved with anyone now even if she wanted to. And Richard's rejection had hurt her deeply. It had also opened her eyes. If a man wanted a family, she couldn't get involved with him.

Lexa crossed her legs under the table. Her knee brushed Josh's. The look in his eyes made her search for a safe subject to discuss.

"Do you and Clare always have such a . . . volatile relationship?"

"If we can't talk things out, we shout them out." His grin spread across his lips. "It's always been that way."

She and her father hadn't had a meaningful conversation in years, and they'd certainly never shouted at each other. Maybe the Flannigans' Irish temperaments had something to do with it.

"Why did you open a job counseling service?" Josh asked nonchalantly.

Lexa could see through his questions. He still wasn't sure about her relationship with Clare. Maybe if she answered them, she could put his mind at ease. "When I was in college, I worked as a girl Friday in a social services office. The system is overloaded, overworked, bogged down in red tape. But what I had learned for myself was reinforced—work gives dignity and pride."

"That's not merely a theory to you, is it?"

His eyes caught hers, trapped them, and compelled her to answer. "No. My dad wouldn't let me work when I was in high school. I felt he was denying me a right."

"Why didn't he want you to work?"

"I don't know. He said he worked hard to provide for us, and we should take advantage of it . . . enjoy being young. But I wanted a job. Anything. The summer after freshman year at college, I took a waitressing job."

"How did your father react?"

Josh's interest seemed genuine. "He couldn't or wouldn't understand my motivation. He couldn't understand why I didn't want to spend the summer at the country club swimming and playing tennis like Dani—my sister. But I didn't want to do that."

"Is your sister older or younger?"

"Younger." And she'd always been a handful. Lexa had seen her through more crises than she wanted to count.

One of the patrons put change in the jukebox. The strains of a popular ballad spilled from the speaker over her head.

Josh wiped his mouth with his napkin and pushed his plate away. Then he leaned back and asked, "Would you like to dance?"

Lexa considered for a moment. Dancing with Joshua Flannigan could be very risky business. Should she take the risk?

Chapter Three

Josh was taking a risk and he knew it. He was attracted to Lexa though he still didn't understand what she was all about. But she touched him. He wanted to hold her in his arms. So this was an experiment. Possibly a dangerous one, but an experiment nonetheless.

She started to shake her head. "I really should get home."

He stood and held out his hand. "One dance."

Lexa took Josh's hand, stood, and let him guide her away from the table.

He surrounded her with his arm while he tucked her hand into his chest. His cheek brushed her hair and he caught his breath. She was soft, perfumed, feminine. So feminine his senses reeled. It had been a long while since he'd held a woman like this. For the past few years, the experience hadn't seemed worth the trouble.

His body tightened. Uh-oh. This experiment was turning serious. He released her slightly and leaned back to look into her incredibly brown eyes. "Do you do this often?"

"What? Dance with a strange man in a bar?"

He grinned. "I beg your pardon. This is not a bar, it's a pub. And I'm certainly not a strange man, though you'd better not ask Clare her opinion. If I were strange, I'm sure you wouldn't be dancing with me.''

As his thighs brushed against hers and his chest grazed her breasts, he saw her swallow hard. She asked, "Is dancing what we're doing?"

He dipped her back until she almost lost her balance and then pulled her up. "Yep. That's what we're doing— dancing. Relax and enjoy the music."

Who was he to tell her to relax? Josh thought. He must be crazy. With his body pressed against hers, her breath quickening, the intoxicating experience of having a soft, lovely woman in his arms, how could *he* relax?

He closed his eyes for a moment, simply enjoying the sensation he knew he'd have to soon bring to an end. She was a career woman, a busy woman. He wanted scads of children and a wife who would enjoy taking care of them. He was beginning to believe that elusive lady was a figment of his imagination.

Their bodies melded magically, moved smoothly, became acquainted. He rubbed his chin along her ear. "You're a very sexy lady."

She was responding to him and he wanted to keep her responding. He wanted to kiss that beautiful, curvy pink mouth . . .

Damn! What was he doing? He didn't know her. She didn't know him. This could only lead one place and though that might be satisfactory for one night, it wasn't what he was searching for.

She must have sensed his change in mood. Raising her head, her gaze asked what he wanted.

Hell if he knew.

She pulled her hand from his and stepped away. "I really have to go."

He didn't disagree. He took her coat from the hanger and held it for her. Like before. Only this time he didn't touch her. "You'll have to let me give you a tour of The Toy Tank sometime."

"Sure." She looked as if she wasn't certain it was a good idea.

Josh left money on their table for their bill and tip and

escorted Lexa to the door. There was an awkwardness between them that hadn't been there before. He didn't like it.

As they walked back to the senior center, he said, "I saw Clare's property today."

"You mean Friendship House?"

Josh chuckled. "So they've named it."

"What did you think?"

The contractor had informed him the structure was sound, the insulation was adequate, the siding provided an almost maintenance-free exterior. The roof should last another five years. "It's big. Four bedrooms."

"But there are three people. They'll fill it. You're still not sold on the idea, are you?"

"It's a big decision. And with the economy the way it is, Clare might not be able to sell her share if she wants out."

"She might never want to sell it."

That was true. Clare could live out the rest of her life happy and content in the old house. He was beginning to think about that possibility.

At Lexa's car, Josh waited for her to unlock her door. "Remember, you have one free pass to tour The Toy Tank anytime."

She smiled. "I'll remember."

Josh shut the door for her once she was inside. Waiting until she turned the key in the ignition, he stepped away. Then he watched as she drove out of the parking lot.

Would he see her again?

Lexa pushed Josh's doorbell for the second time. Maybe she should just leave. The store manager had told her that Josh had left for the day. But Clare had told Lexa he lived in the apartment above the store.

Lexa had thought about Josh for the past four days. She'd fully intended not to see him again. He could only make her life more complicated. But she'd intended to visit The Toy Tank anyway to see what she could use for the baby. And it would have been rude not to stop and say hello, wouldn't it?

Lexa jabbed the doorbell a third time. Maybe he'd already left. She sighed with relief and turned away, ready to descend the steps.

The door swung open and she stared in amazement.

Josh stood in front of her, hair sopping wet. Droplets of water dotted his broad bare shoulders, caught in swirls of black hair on his chest. His hand clutched a blue towel low on his hips. It didn't begin to cover his powerful thighs.

"Lexa!"

His hand went to the end of the towel tucked at his waist. "Come on in." When she hesitated, he took a few steps back. "Come on. You can make yourself comfortable. I just have to rinse off the rest of the soap. Give me five minutes."

She stepped over the threshold, trying not to stare at his bare chest.

Waving her into the expansive living room, Josh disappeared down a narrow hall that led to what she assumed was the bedroom.

Looking around curiously, she studied the man through his decor. A whimsical mobile of unicorns dangled in one corner. The long sofa and chair trimmed with dark pine were covered in a beige and navy quilted material. Some type of board game and assorted magazines were spread on the narrow cobbler's bench. Navy blue drapes were drawn across the windows. Lexa wondered how often Josh used the miniature basketball backboard and net that stood in one corner. She sank down on the chair next to a three-foot-high gum ball machine and smiled.

She liked everything she knew about Josh. It was a shame they couldn't . . . She remembered the pain when Richard had said to her, "I love you. But I want children. And if you can't give them to me, we don't have a future." When she'd brought up adoption, he'd said, "I want my *own* children."

He'd walked out. She'd been so hurt, so angry. And the rejection still hurt. Sometimes she only felt like half a woman. She tried to tell herself that wasn't so. She tried to tell herself the right man could accept her as she was.

Why was she even thinking about it? She was simply going to tour a toy store.

If Josh wasn't on his way out.

Lexa stood when she heard his footsteps in the hallway. His oxford shirt was open at the collar, the sleeves rolled up. The black corduroy slacks hugged his hips almost as seductively as his jeans. With his hair still damp, he was as sexy as a poster idol.

"Did you come for the grand tour?"

"Yes, but if you're busy . . . "

He grinned. "Nope."

He didn't bother with a coat, but led her out the door, down the steps, and around to the front of the store like an anxious boy eager to show off his prized possession.

As they strolled down the aisles, Josh smiled at the employees they passed and the few remaining customers. Lexa stopped to look at a display of crystals a child could grow in a dish pan, a telescope powerful enough to see the craters on the moon in detail, an ant farm with live ants. There were the usual toddler toys, blocks, and stuffed animals, plus sundry electronics kits, roller skates, and books for older children.

But what really caught her attention were the crib mobiles hanging from fixtures on the top shelf. She stopped to examine one made of cloth. Animals floated from a circus big top. Thinking out loud, she said, "I like the ones with music boxes."

Josh took her elbow and led her to another section of the shelf. "Look at this one." He wound the center and Brahms' "Lullaby" played sweetly. As Lexa checked the shapes on the mobile, Josh took a box from the stack and shook off the lid. "This mobile changes with the child."

Lexa picked up a plastic ball with a textured surface.

Josh explained, "The pieces are interchangeable. Every few months, you change them to meet the child's developmental stages. More color, more texture, more interest. And look at these busy boxes."

Lexa reached for a toy that could hang on the playpen or crib. When she flipped a lever, a clown popped up. When she slid a piece of plastic to one side, it revealed a mirror on the other. She pushed a button and the toy mooed like a cow.

She laughed. "This is terrific. I'll have to—" She stopped.

"Do you have someone you want to buy this for? We have different types. I can show you the others."

She laid the busy box on its display holder. "No. Thanks."

Josh gave her a long look. When she didn't say anything more, he pointed to table displaying radio-controlled cars. "Let me show you my favorite."

Lexa wondered if she'd made a mistake coming here today. Josh was almost too likable for her peace of mind. He didn't just own a toy store. He *enjoyed* owning a toy store.

Josh picked up a display model that looked like a black Jaguar with orange markings. He crouched on the floor and pressed the control. The car veered to the right, slightly to the left, then zoomed down the long aisle at top speed.

Lexa hopped out of the way. "I didn't know they could go that fast!"

Josh stood, the control still in hand. "That was slow. You should see us race them."

"Us?"

"I'm the moderator for a radio car club. The kids get together twice a month and race their cars."

Kids. He did like kids or he wouldn't spend his free time with them. He liked kids and toys and . . .

"Lexa?"

"What?" She suddenly realized she'd missed a question.

"Would you like to come watch sometime? As long as the weather holds, we race them in the back lot."

"Here?"

"Um-hm. In the winter we borrow a school gymnasium. Next year I don't know what we'll do." He pushed a button and the car came back toward him.

"Why? Is there a problem?"

"I've started talking with a contractor about expanding the store. We'll be adding on in the back and it will cut the macadam space in half." Josh picked up the car and put it on the table.

"Business is that good? I thought all retail sales were down."

Josh stooped down and picked up the car. "Maybe it's because we're smaller than the chains, but with seasonal incentives and our new party planner campaign, we're doing great."

"What's a party planner?"

"Well, I had this idea but I wasn't sure it would work. So I tried it out on my manager and we decided to experiment. We have a register of sorts on the computer. A parent comes to us with a list so all the child's friends and relatives know what he wants and they don't duplicate presents or buy something that has to be returned. And then we give a package deal on party plans. For instance, if they want a Ninja Turtles theme, we coordinate paper goods, prizes, favors, balloons. We've been doing this for six months and the response has been unbelievable."

"Who takes care of all this?"

"I have two people who coordinate it all. I'll have to put somebody else on it for Christmas, maybe two. We're going to try the lists for Christmas and see how it goes. Stores who give personal service have an edge on the market these days because service is hard to find. And if the last six months are any indication, next year at this time I'll be thinking about an addition to the Harrisburg store."

When they turned down another aisle, Josh pulled a box from a shelf and grinned mischievously. "This just came in. Come into the back with me and we'll try it out."

"Can't we try it here?"

"You'll be safe with me in the storeroom," he kidded. "I promise I'll leave the lights on."

She laughed. "You bet you will or I'll tell Clare." The idea of her and Josh in a dark storeroom gave her a pleasant shiver. As she gazed into his eyes, the connection between them was too strong to ignore.

But she did her best and lowered her gaze to the box in his hands.

His voice was husky. "You have to set this on a flat surface. Let's try it out."

The storeroom was a large area with stacks and stacks of shelves, cartons as yet unpacked, stray toys that were defective or damaged. Josh set the box on a workbench against the wall and pulled out the wooden box inside.

"It's called Space Tilt," he explained, taking a small silver ball out of a plastic bag and setting it on the number one. A movable piece of plastic with maze-like grooves and lines was set on top of a wooden frame. The object was to move the ball from numbers one to thirty-five by tilting the board and making sure the ball would travel along the lines, avoiding the holes.

Lexa put her purse on the workbench and said, "You go first and show me how it works."

Josh positioned the ball and began tilting. He made it to number eleven before the ball dropped down a hole. "I made it to twenty yesterday. I must have lost my touch."

"Do you practice often?" She had the feeling this was a habit.

He raised his hand in a Boy Scout pledge position. "I must confess, I try out many of the toys before we sell them. How else do I know what to reorder?"

She laughed and took her turn at tilting. The ball fell in the hole at number five. "It's not as easy as it looks. Let me try again."

He chuckled. "I warn you, it's addictive. You keep attempting to beat your own score."

It *was* addictive. The more Lexa tried it, the more she wanted to try again. As soon as she was able to match Josh's skill, she and Josh took turns. Josh had reached twenty-three and Lexa nineteen when Josh looked at his watch. "We've been at this an hour. You must be starved!" He let his eyes wander from the lapels of her wine-colored suit to her gray kid pumps. "Let alone uncomfortable. I don't see how women wear those high heels."

"I'm used to them. But my toes are beginning to pinch." She checked her watch. "I do have to go."

"Have supper with me. I can whip up some omelets—a salad."

Oh, how she'd like to. She hadn't enjoyed time with a man this much in years. But she couldn't. Not safely. If she stayed, she might want to stay longer. "I can't. But thanks for the tour. You really love the store, don't you?"

"Business management can be a dry field. I wanted to use my skills with something I enjoy. I didn't want to dread coming to work. And I don't. Ever." He winked. "Besides, owning the store will be great when I have five kids and can bring home the toys at a wholesale price."

Five kids. She'd been right about him. That meant he was wrong for her. She smiled politely. "Well, thanks again for the tour. If I know anyone who needs toys, I'll certainly recommend your store."

She retrieved her purse from the worktable. "Say hello to Clare if you see her before I do."

He nodded. "I'll walk you to the door."

Lexa walked beside him, aware of his appeal, his rugged handsomeness, her attraction to him. And she told herself she knew what was best for both of them.

Lexa entered her apartment Monday evening and dropped her briefcase on the floor with a tired sigh. She needed to catch up on sleep from the weekend. She and Dani had talked late into the night Saturday. Her sister and Rob had broken up for good. Lexa sighed. Dani was unhappy without him. She was young and in love and didn't want that love to end. Her pregnancy was a reminder the love hadn't been strong enough to survive.

But Dani was sure about the adoption. She didn't want to raise the baby alone.

Lexa went into the kitchen for a glass of juice and her phone rang. She picked up quickly.

"Lexa, it's Clare."

Lexa smiled. "Are you moved?"

"Moved but not unpacked."

"I can help if you'd like."

"Josh is coming over tomorrow night."

"Uh, I'm busy tomorrow."

"But I need to talk to you *and* Josh."

Lexa sighed inaudibly. She didn't want to see Josh again. She didn't want anything to start between them. She had the feeling it could.

But if Clare had a problem. . .

"What time would you like me to be there?"

"We'll have a potluck supper. Come around six. Or is that too early?"

"No. My last appointment is four-thirty. I'll come after that."

Lexa said goodbye to Clare and hung up the phone. There was no earthly reason why she and Josh couldn't be friendly.

Lexa mounted the steps to Clare's new house. It was sixty years old and nestled between tall spruce trees set far back from the street.

She lifted the knocker and let it fall twice. When no one answered, she tried the knob, found it unlocked, and stepped into the long living room.

Josh was arguing with his aunt. "I told you I'd hang the drapes."

Clare glowered at him from the three-foot step ladder. "You were busy replacing the light fixture upstairs."

"Can't stay out of trouble, can you?"

Lexa felt awkward, overhearing.

Clare looked up and saw her. "Lexa! Good. Now you can help me keep Josh in line. What am I going to do with him? He keeps treating me as if I were ninety-nine, frail, and an invalid."

"I do not. I just want you to use your common sense."

"My common sense and yours must be different."

Josh let out a frustrated sigh. "Will you please get down from the ladder?"

"I'm not finished."

Lexa crossed to them and said softly, "She has two more pins to clip. You could hold the ladder steady until she does."

Josh didn't look as if he appreciated her interference.

But he did as she suggested. He asked his aunt, "Are there any more drapes to hang?"

Clare gave the curtains a critical look and climbed down. "No. Everything's done except to bring a few boxes from my bedroom to the living room. I can do that tomorrow. Jim and Trudy will help me unpack."

Josh shook his head with affectionate exasperation. "What am I going to do with you?"

"Put up with me because I'm not going to change."

Lexa laughed. "Score one for Clare."

Josh suppressed a smile and held her eyes with his. "Whose side are you on?"

"Does anybody ever win these go-arounds?" Lexa asked, taking off her jacket and laying it over a stack of boxes.

"I do," they chorused in unison.

Clare closed the stepladder and leaned it against the wall. "I made barbecued hamburgers and pasta salad. I hope you're in the mood for a picnic."

"What can we do?" Lexa asked.

"Follow me to the kitchen."

Josh motioned in front of him. "Ladies first."

Lexa had tried to forget the quicksilver sparkle that danced in his eyes.

The kitchen was a bright room with birch cabinets and blue-checked café curtains at the windows. Clare took a vinyl tablecloth from a drawer in the dry sink and spread it over the maple table. "Josh, get the food out of the refrigerator. Lexa, silverware is in the drawer beside the sink."

As Josh went to the refrigerator, Lexa passed in front of him. Her hip brushed his. Their gazes met. Lord, he seemed to see right through her. Flustered, she turned away and pulled out the drawer. She'd find out what Clare wanted, eat, and run. She did have to make a few calls.

"So, Clare. Why did you need to see me and Josh?" She looked at Josh. "Or do you already know?"

He set a tray of fresh vegetables and a casserole of pasta salad on the table. "No, we've been too busy to talk."

Clare smoothed out creases in the tablecloth. "Lexa, do

you know anything about the financial advisor who talked to the seniors?''

Lexa grabbed napkins from the pack lying on the counter. ''I went to see him the next day to find out his qualifications. He said he graduated from Temple with a degree in accounting. There was a diploma on the wall, but something about him doesn't ring true.''

''Mary was here this afternoon. She was thinking about investing money from CDs that were up for renewal. She went to Mr. Stanley to see what he thought. He advised her against it. He proposed she put her money into an adult community. Leisureville, he called it.''

''What does he mean by an adult community?'' Josh's gaze met Lexa's. This time it was concerned.

''There are a couple around here, but this one's in Florida. It's just getting started. There's a swimming pool, tennis, shuffleboard, a social club. There are plans to start another in South Carolina and Texas, too. She can invest as little as two thousand dollars or as much as she wants. And if she invests now, she gets her name on a list. If she wants to buy one of the houses, she would get first choice.''

Josh inclined his head and leaned against the counter. ''Her investment doesn't buy her anything?''

Clare took plates from the cabinet beside the sink. ''No. Her investment is an investment. Stanley says she'll earn more interest than she could hope to get on CDs, a money market account, or a mutual fund.''

Lexa had been listening carefully as she placed silverware in their proper setting at the small dinette table. ''I'm surprised he recommended that. She can't afford to risk her money at her age.''

Josh shrugged. ''Maybe it's not a risk. Maybe it's fairly safe. If it's run by a stable corporation, it would be like a corporate bond.''

''But the safety of the bond depends on the stability of the corporation issuing them. I'd like to know the name of the company so it could be checked out with a rating service.''

''What's that?'' Clare put a plate at each setting.

Josh explained before Lexa had the chance. ''There are

rating services that evaluate the credit rating of a corporation.''

''But wouldn't Mr. Stanley have done that?'' Clare looked perplexed.

Lexa took the plastic wrap from the food Josh had brought to the table. ''I would hope so. But I don't understand his thinking. Why not treasury bills? Or municipal bonds? They're safe and free from income tax.''

Josh fished serving spoons from a drawer. ''I have a friend who's a detective in the police department. Maybe he can make a check on Stanley and find out if he's legitimate. There are con artists out there who prey on the elderly.''

Lexa was glad Josh wasn't dismissing his aunt's concerns. And with a contact in the police department, he could probably get farther than she could.

Supper with Josh and Clare was an experience for Lexa. Josh and his aunt laughed, argued, and joked freely with no undercurrents or hostilities. It was different from her own family. When she went home, she and Dani ate quietly with their father and engaged only in polite conversation. Lexa was worried how her father was going to take the news that Dani was pregnant.

Josh watched Lexa as she spoke with him without meeting his eyes, as she talked with Clare as if they'd been friends for years. She was an enigma.

She'd turned up at the store for a tour. He'd been surprised how much that pleased him. Of course the way he'd been dressed, or rather, undressed . . . Her eyes on him had made his pulse gallop, his body throb. How often could simply a woman's gaze do that?

He still didn't know exactly what had happened at the store, though he could make a good guess. He'd mentioned five kids, wanting a big family. And she'd gotten as nervous as a scared rabbit. She was a career woman, all right. The thought of diapers and teething rings probably seemed dreary and unexciting. Though she'd been interested in infants' toys.

He definitely couldn't figure her out.

* * *

After they'd finished supper and cleaned up the kitchen, Lexa went to the living room for her jacket. She'd been very careful not to get too close to him. Josh wondered if that was because she felt the same electricity he did.

When she said goodbye to Clare, Josh decided to tempt fate. "I'll walk you to your car."

"That's not necessary."

"I could use some fresh air. Clare, I'll be back in a few minutes."

"Take your time." His aunt gave him a wicked grin that had matchmaker stamped from one end to the other. She turned to Lexa and hugged her. "I'll see you at the Halloween party if not before."

Lexa and Josh stepped outside into the crisp autumn air. Stray leaves flittered in the breeze. Josh walked with Lexa down the curved path cutting through the yard. "Did you have a good weekend with your sister?"

"It was nice."

"Are you close?"

Lexa smiled. "Yes. We're as different as night and day. But we've always had each other."

"The two of you against the world?"

She nodded, hesitated, then said, "Dani and I had problems with our stepmother. So that made our bond even stronger."

Josh stood on the sidewalk with Lexa, entranced with the gold in her hair shimmering under the streetlight's glow. "Are you going to the Halloween party by yourself?"

"Yes."

"I could pick you up."

"I don't think that's a good idea."

"Why not?"

She ducked her head and took her keys from her purse. "It just isn't." She turned away to open her car door.

Deciding to confront her head-on, Josh clasped her shoulder. "Lexa, why are you running from me?"

Chapter Four

"I'm not running." Lexa could feel the heat of each of Josh's fingers burning through her jacket and blouse.

"Then go to the Halloween party with me."

Lexa knew she shouldn't. She suspected the more time she spent with Josh, the more time she'd want to spend with him. How had she gotten herself into this mess? She looked up at him and that was a mistake. His honest blue eyes enticed and excited her.

"All right. I'll go with you. But . . . "

"But?"

"But I can't get involved with anyone right now. If we go, we go as friends."

His gaze was filled with questions he didn't ask. Maybe because he guessed she wouldn't answer them. He smiled. "That sounds good to me."

Yes, friendship sounded good, Lexa thought as she poured herself a cup of punch. But deep down, she knew more than friendship was simmering between her and Josh.

They'd arrived an hour ago and had been socializing

most of that time with Clare and her friends. Lexa felt very safe . . . until she looked at Josh. History had never seen a handsomer or sexier Dracula. His long legs encased in slim black trousers, the black turtleneck hugging his chest, the dramatic black cape trimmed in red. He'd discarded the mask soon after they'd arrived.

The disc jockey was playing songs from the forties, fifties, and sixties. Lexa took a sip of punch.

A hand on her shoulder startled her.

Josh took her hand. "Let's see you jitterbug, gypsy."

She and Josh quickly matched their basic step and began. Her full red skirt swirled around her when he twirled her; her white satin blouse clung as he spun her, guided her, pulled her into a sidecar position and swept her in a circle. When the dance was over, he pulled her to him and gave her a giant hug. "You were terrific."

His damp heat met hers and locked her to him. Her arms had automatically circled his back to return the hug. She felt his belt buckle against her stomach, she smelled intoxicating male, and when she gazed into his eyes, she wanted to stroke his face. Impossible. Totally impossible. Where *was* her common sense?

She pulled out of his embrace and fanned herself with her hand.

"Need a breath of fresh air?"

"Sounds good."

They were standing outside only a few moments when Lexa realized fall was gone and winter was making its entrance, at least after the sun went down. She shivered.

"Do you want to go back in?"

Lexa took a few deep breaths, needing the sense-clearing of the colder air. "No. Not yet."

"Lexa, I want to see you again."

"Josh . . . "

"Give me a good reason why we shouldn't have fun together as we have tonight."

"You don't understand my life. I have commitments and I take them all seriously."

"So do I." After an uncomfortable pause, Josh pushed a few of Lexa's curls away from her brow. So much passion.

So much caring. Why? Yes, she was a busy woman and he'd sworn never again to get involved with someone like that. But she seemed to know how to play and have fun, too. She wasn't all work.

He wanted to get to know Lexa, to explore the vibrations humming every time they talked, every time they touched. "I know what you do is important. Look at the difference the senior center has made in Clare's life. Did you see her dancing with Jim in there? I haven't seen her this happy in years."

"You *do* understand."

He caressed her cheek. "I do. So what do you say? What are your plans next weekend?"

"I'm going to Penn State to see Dani."

"When will you be back?"

"Sunday afternoon."

If he put the power in her hands, maybe she'd understand he didn't want to box her in. "Call me when you get back. Maybe we can go to dinner or something."

She still hesitated.

He tipped her chin up with his knuckle. "I want to see you again."

He leaned forward. Her stunning brown eyes were wide with indecision. Her mouth was slightly parted. Her soft hair curled enticingly around her pretty face. Desire, strong and potent, surged through him. But he sensed if he pushed, Lexa would be gone.

Instead of bending his head and exploring her lips, he dropped a light kiss on her forehead and backed away.

She looked confused. "Josh, if I don't call Sunday, it's not because I don't like you."

His brows hiked up. "It's because . . . "

"My life's complicated right now."

At this moment, he wanted to be one of the complications. He'd give her the space she needed . . . for a while. But if she didn't call Sunday, he'd try again.

Lexa plopped her overnight case in her bedroom and stared at the phone by her bed. Should she call Josh? Dare she? Could he possibly want to get involved with a woman who was going to adopt a baby? A woman who couldn't have her own children?

She looked up his number in the phone book and dialed. Josh picked it up immediately. "Hello?"

"It's Lexa. I'm back." She wished she could see his face. "Uh, do you still want to get together?"

"Get together. That has a world of possibilities," he teased.

Her stomach fluttered.

"Lexa? Of course, I want to get together. Do you have a backyard?"

"What?"

"A backyard. Do you have one?"

"Yes. But why?"

"Is it big?"

"It's long and narrow."

"Great. I have a new toy to try out. I'll be right over."

"Do you know where I live?"

"I checked the phone book. I don't need directions. I'll be there in fifteen minutes."

After Lexa said goodbye, she felt as if she had been caught in a revolving door. He had so much energy, seemed to know exactly what he wanted to do, where he wanted to go. She remembered him saying, "When I have five kids . . . " Had she made a mistake calling him?

When Lexa heard a car pull into the driveway to her town house, she peeked out the window. She saw Josh looking at something in his trunk. She pulled her suede jacket out of the closet and went outside. His taste in cars was classy—a two-toned burgundy Buick Electra. Josh was gathering cellophane packages out of his trunk that looked as if they contained pieces of long white Styrofoam.

He tucked the packages under one arm and slammed the trunk. When he saw her, he smiled—one of those devastating smiles that weakened her knees. She felt inordinately happy to see him. "What do you have?"

He draped his arm around her shoulders as if he had been doing it all his life and walked beside her. "They're gliders. They operate on a boomerang principle. If you fly them correctly, they come back to you."

She could feel the strength in his arm, the strength in him. "How far do they fly?"

"Twenty or thirty feet. At least that's what the instructions say."

They crossed the front yard and walked along the side of the house to the back. Lexa glanced at the packages under his arm. "Instructions. Does that mean we have to put them together?"

He shrugged. "They're supposed to be easy to assemble. We don't have to paste on the decals before their maiden voyages."

Josh and Lexa sat on the back porch steps and ripped open the packages. Lexa watched Josh maneuver the wing across the body of the glider.

He glanced at her and asked, "How was your visit with your sister?"

"It was fine." Lexa wished she could tell Josh all about it. It would be wonderful to be able to confide in someone the way Dani confided in her.

Josh didn't press her further but assembled his glider. "How's yours coming?"

She wiggled the wings of the plane into the body. "It looks like yours."

They stood and walked to the middle of the yard. Autumn danced all around them from the orange and crimson leaves on the tall maples to the brisk breeze that hinted at a November wind.

Josh held up his hand, crossed his fingers, and gave her a heart-stopping grin. Then he sent the glider on a test run. A gust of wind made it veer crazily and crash.

"This is going to take practice," he called as he chased after it.

Lexa tried to follow the directions, to fly the plane in a certain arc, but hers, too, fell on the grass. She and Josh chased back and forth for a half hour until Lexa found exactly the right combination of wrist movements.

When the glider arched, dove, and came back to her, she caught it in one hand. "I did it!"

Josh approached her and stood at her elbow. "Now you can teach me."

Josh watched Lexa's face instead of her hands. He seemed to be trying to see into her soul. When he reached out and ran his thumb along her cheekbone, she trembled. She'd never reacted like this to a man and it scared her to death.

The sun was setting and the shadows were long. The turquoise sky had become shot through with purple, rose, and orange.

"It's beautiful, isn't it?" she murmured. "Sunsets are like the ocean. When I look at them, feel surrounded by them, in awe of them, I almost feel like crying."

"I understand. I feel the same way."

Instead of the sunset, she looked at him. "I'm surprised. Men usually make fun of that kind of thinking. Or call it sentimental."

"It's not sentimental to appreciate artistry and beauty. Listening to a symphony can evoke the same feeling. I don't know why most men are afraid of that. But I believe if they're afraid of that, they're afraid of love. It comes from the same source."

Josh wasn't only fun. He was special. "Have you ever cried?" For a moment, she didn't think he was going to answer her.

Then he said quietly, "Yes. I cried when my parents died. I had a good friend who had to have his leg amputated. I cried with him and for him. There have been moments when I could have cried but didn't because of the people around me. I knew they'd never understand. I guess I wasn't mature enough then to have the freedom to be myself."

She shifted her glider from one hand to the other. "I know what you mean, but I don't know how men control their tears. I'm the type who cries at *Bambi* and 'reach out and touch someone' commercials."

"That means you know your emotions and you're not afraid to express them. I bet other people's emotions don't scare you, do they?"

"I've never thought about it, but I guess they don't."

He took the glider from her hand and laid it on the grass next to his. When he straightened, he rested his hands on her shoulders. "But for some reason, I scare you. Why, Lexa?"

His perception caught her off guard. "I . . . I don't know. I like you, Josh, but there are things you don't know about me."

"I have plenty of time to find out what they are if you let me in."

"Josh, I'm not sure—"

"Maybe this will help you be sure."

He bent his head and slowly lowered his mouth to hers. He began softly but with firm pressure. After a few moments, his tongue teased back and forth along her lips.

Lexa's heart fluttered like a trapped hummingbird. Her hand moved from his shoulder to the back of his neck. As his tongue sweetly probed, her fingers played in his hair.

He kissed like a man who knew how to love, knew how to touch and wanted to be touched in return. She'd been kissed before. All kinds of kisses—beard-scratching kisses, invitation-to-bed kisses, weak kisses, domineering kisses. But Josh's kiss was lyrical, gentle yet masterful, giving yet taking, and evocative, so evocative. It wasn't just his lips and tongue, but the tenderness of his hold, the exciting unfamiliarity of his long, strong body.

Josh's hand released hers and caressed the side of her face. She sighed and his tongue became more seductive, encouraging hers to play. Finally, he slowed down and ended the kiss.

Lexa stared up at him, disoriented, aroused, and embarrassed. "We shouldn't have done that." She didn't know if she was trying to convince him or herself.

His voice was husky. "Why not?"

"Because . . . because it confused me. I'm not usually like this."

"Let's try it again and maybe it will unconfuse you," he suggested with a renegade smile.

She pulled her arms from around his neck and placed her hands on his chest in case he might try.

His eyes seemed to swallow her as he gathered her close

to him again. The only place to put her arms was around his neck. His lips sealed to hers. His tongue asked her to open. This kiss was pure feeling, pure passion, a coming together.

Lexa's world spun and she hung on to Josh for support. The slight prickle of his beard, the fragrance of his cologne, the heat of his lips, the skill of his tongue intoxicated her.

Josh's tongue tempted hers to reciprocate. When she did, he took her deeper into his mouth. She yielded to him and became soft in his arms. The hesitancy was gone.

His control slipped away until he caressed her back, quested lower and kneaded her roundness, pushing her into his hips. But it wasn't enough. His right hand slipped under her jacket. His palm molded her sweater to her breast as he felt for her nipple under the fabric. It was hard and he could imagine flicking it with his tongue. He swore to himself. He had to stop this and he had to stop it *now*.

Josh became harder as Lexa melted into him. She had never felt more fully her power as a woman. The heart of her womanhood tensed, coiled, heated, until she thought she'd explode. When his hand touched her breast, she felt the rippling from her fingers to her toes. Is this what making love with Josh would be like? Not mechanical. Not rote. But dynamic, free-flowing, a road to heaven.

His hand dropped, his hold loosened, his lips clung for a moment and then released. Her body cried out "Why?" but her mind answered, *Because she had to stop*. She could never give Josh what he wanted.

Josh framed her cheeks with his hands. "I'm sorry, Lexa. I didn't mean for that to get so out of hand."

"It wasn't your fault." Tears pricked in her eyes.

He must have seen them. "Was I wrong? Didn't you want that as much as I did?"

"It was . . . overwhelming."

He smiled. "I know. Lexa, I think we have something right we should explore. Don't you?"

"I'm not ready."

She turned and fled, unable to face the wondering hurt in his eyes.

Chapter Five

It was almost four o'clock when Lexa parked her compact among the shoppers' cars in The Toy Tank's parking lot and walked around to the back. She had to tell him about Dani before things went any further. She had waited too long. The bewildered look on his face when she'd last seen him was clear and painful evidence of that. She crossed to the course indicated by fluorescent orange pylons and tin cans where Josh was crouched down next to a little boy about eight years old. They were both holding a radio-controlled car. Tears were running down the child's cheeks. Josh was comforting him and patting his shoulder.

Lexa stopped a few feet away and heard Josh say, "Your car ran a *terrific* race. It beat mine. Maybe next time it will win."

The tears stopped and the child's expression was hopeful. "Do you really think so?"

Josh stood and looked down at the child affectionately. "I really think so."

A car pulled into the parking lot and the driver honked the horn. The little boy grinned, waved at Josh, and ran to the waiting car, yelling, "I'll see you next time."

Josh waved back and called after him, "You keep practicing. You're getting really good."

Lexa's heart contracted. She had suspected Josh would be good with children.

He straightened, and appraised her forest green suit, stopping at its rather abbreviated hem.

"Hello. Nice to see you."

The desire in his eyes lent a sensual force to his words.

She shifted on her high heels, and gestured to the car on the macadam to distract him. "How do they run?"

It took him more than a moment to take his eyes off her legs, but he managed. "They're not complicated. How would you like to learn how to race a radio-controlled car?"

"My father wouldn't teach me how to drive because he said he didn't have enough patience. If this is anything like driving, you might want to think twice before offering."

"I'm a great teacher," Josh assured her.

She bet he was. She could imagine him teaching her about making love with him. She switched her attention to the course around them. "If you can teach me how to maneuver through that obstacle course, you're a superior teacher."

He stooped over and picked up the model Toyota. "This car has a three-point suspension system with front coil springs."

Her look was blank. "Is that important?"

He chuckled. "It is for an RC enthusiast, but not for you."

"Good," she said. "Because I'm a 'show me' person. If you tell me, I probably won't get it right. If you show me, I will."

His eyes twinkled mischievously. "I could show you lots of things."

She picked up his meaning all too well.

"Now I know why Clare insists you're incorrigible."

He laughed. "Yep. That's one of her words. It's a hard reputation to maintain."

Lexa bit back a smile as Josh maneuvered the car along

the course. He offered her the control. "Here, you take it. Doing is learning."

"Sometimes it's better to learn first."

"Not with this. Go ahead and try it."

She moved the joystick, tentatively trying to coordinate the speed with the motion.

The car surged ahead and ran into a pylon. "Don't worry. Back it up," Josh advised.

Lexa slowly guided the car around a curve.

"The idea is to avert the obstacles and complete the course in the least amount of time."

She zoomed the car ahead and sideswiped a tin can. Josh wrapped his arms around her with her back resting against his chest. With one hand, he covered her fingers to help guide the model. With the other, he pointed to the car. "Keep your eyes on the area in front of the car. If you only watch the car, you can't keep clear of the obstacles."

It felt so good to have his arms around her. She took a deep breath, relishing the feel of him, the closeness. But she couldn't get any closer unless she was honest with him.

Lexa's hands went still and the car stopped. She turned in Josh's arms, control box in hand, until she faced him. "Josh, there's something I have to tell you."

"What?"

"Dani's pregnant, and I'm going to adopt her baby."

Josh was still for a stunned moment, his eyes wide with surprise. When he spoke, it wasn't what she expected. "So *that's* why you've been backing off."

"It's not something I could just blurt out to a stranger."

"Am I a stranger, Lexa?"

"No. Not anymore. That's why I had to tell you." She cleared her throat. "So how do you feel about it?"

His smile was uncertain. "It's a shock."

She hadn't known what to expect. His reaction wasn't negative exactly, but he wasn't telling her what she needed to know. She'd simply have to ask straight out. "Do you still want to see me?"

He took her by the shoulders. "Of course, I still want to see you. Why wouldn't I?"

She murmured, "Some men would find a baby hard to accept."

"I'm not *some* men. And don't forget, kids are my business."

True, Lexa thought, but owning a toy store and liking kids was not the same as being a father.

He must have seen her doubts. "Lexa, if you had ten kids, I'd still want to see you again."

Relief seeped through her and she wanted to hug him. "Really?"

"Really. But I can certainly understand why you don't want to rush into anything. You're thinking about someone other than yourself."

"Josh, any type of relationship has to be strong to support a child. I have to be absolutely certain . . ."

"That I'm the right guy?" he filled in. He gently rubbed up and down her arms. "I understand. Believe me, I do. Is your sister sure she doesn't want to keep the baby?"

Josh's hands scorched through her suit jacket. The motion was meant to be comforting, but it was arousing instead. "She's positive. Her boyfriend deserted her. She wants to have the baby but she says she can't raise it alone."

"And you can."

Her eyes didn't waver from his. "I can."

"You're a brave woman."

"Bravery has nothing to do with it. I love Dani; I'll love her baby."

"Maybe you won't have to do it alone."

Apprehension tinged her voice. "It's too soon to make any kind of commitment."

"But it's not too soon to hope in the future," he insisted.

Josh smiled and she smiled back. One bridge successfully crossed. All she needed now was the courage to tell him the rest. But not today. Soon.

As Josh pulled up in front of Lexa's town house, a glare of hidden sun fought the clouds. He'd called Lexa and asked her if she still wanted to go bicycling on the Gettysburg Battlefield with the lower temperatures. She'd insisted she liked to ride in cold weather. The sky looked ominous. They might have to cut the afternoon short.

But that wouldn't bother Josh, not at all. They could go back to his apartment, curl up on the sofa together, let whatever was going to happen, happen. For three weeks, since the day she'd told him about the adoption, he'd kept everything light with Lexa, letting her set the tone. He was "activitied" out. Bowling, the fall craft fair, the recreational vehicle show. Everything to do or see so the chemistry between them didn't explode when they were alone.

He realized Lexa needed time. She was still holding back and he couldn't figure out why. Was it the idea of becoming a mother? Or was it something more? Something she wasn't telling him? He was a firm believer that physical intimacy led to deeper emotional intimacy. And he was ready to deepen their relationship. But Lexa . . .

He was beginning to understand that it was much easier for her to give than to receive. But why did she have to give so much? He respected her causes. He liked the idea of her adopting a child, if she was sure that's what she and her sister wanted. But if their relationship was going to grow, she'd have to give it more time. Today was the day to bring it up. Today was the day he was going to kiss her somewhere quiet, somewhere comfortable. Maybe tonight would be the night.

The red and white pickup truck that pulled into Lexa's driveway had a cover on the back. Josh always thought of everything. He was so much fun, except when he got that serious gleam in his eyes that said he wanted to get closer *now*. She still had doubts.

Would Josh resent the time she spent with a child? And how would he feel when he knew she couldn't have more children? Questions without answers.

Josh was becoming dear to her. Even when they weren't together, he let her know he was thinking about her. One day she'd played back the tape on her answering machine to hear the Beatles' "I Want to Hold Your Hand." Another day he'd sent her a bouquet of daisies. Yesterday she'd received a box of imported chocolates by messenger. She'd never met anyone like him, so tender, gentle, caring. She didn't want to spoil what was developing between them.

Lexa pulled on her down jacket and went from her kitchen to the garage. She pressed a button and her garage door opened. She wheeled her bicycle to the back of Josh's truck.

He was already opening the tailgate. "It's a little cold for a picnic lunch."

"Are you backing out on me, Flannigan?"

"Me? I was just trying to give you a chance to change your mind. Just you wait until we start pedaling up those hills. Then we'll see who wants to back out."

Josh maneuvered around the busy town square in Gettysburg, and headed toward the Battlefield and the National Tower. Red, white, and blue flags flapped in the breeze as he cruised up the driveway to the parking lot. He climbed out of the truck and unloaded the bicycles.

Lexa and Josh rode along the Battlefield's scenic auto route through a portion of the 3,500-acre historic site, stopping at focal points, and exchanging pleasantries with a few tourists. At the Pennsylvania State Monument, they left their bikes and walked up the steps. In silence they examined the life-size bronze statues and the plaques engraved with the names of soldiers who had died in battle.

Lexa's stomach began growling as they walked their bikes up the hill to Devils' Den, a group of giant boulders from which the Union troops had been routed. They climbed up the natural stone steps and explored the village of rock formations. When Lexa's foot slipped on one of the boulders, Josh caught her up against his side.

He held her tightly for a few moments, then released her. When her stomach growled loudly again, he gave her a wry smile. "We'd better head back to the truck. I have a bucket of fried chicken and biscuits." He gazed at the sky that was getting more foreboding by the minute.

When they arrived at the tower, Lexa asked, "Do you think we have time to go up to the top before it rains?"

His eyes met hers and they connected for a moment. "I don't see why not. We might not be able to see very far, though."

"It doesn't matter. I just like being at the top."

Lexa and Josh walked along the timber-lined, macadam path approaching the 393-foot structure. Josh didn't touch her and she wished he would. What was he waiting for?

An elevator with tall glass windows sped them to the observation capsule. They followed a map around the glassed-in deck, turning it clockwise as they walked around the tower and listened to recorded history.

Two more flights of stairs led up to the open observation deck, where a mist was beginning to fall. Wind skipped through their hair as they gazed at white tombstone markers.

Looking back in time, looking at the expanse of blue-gray sky, looking through the gathering fog to see the beyond, Lexa suddenly felt very alone. Tears pricked behind her eyes.

As if he sensed her thought, Josh hung his arm across her shoulders.

His hand ran down the back of her hair. It was becoming softer and curlier in the dampness. His arms encircled her in a nurturing hug. He murmured against her temple, "Let's go back down before we get wet."

They sat comfortably in the truck, the basket of chicken between them. Sleet began pinging against the windshield. Lexa picked up a piece of chicken, and bit into it hungrily. Josh looked at her and grinned.

He swiped a smudge of chicken coating from Lexa's upper lip with his forefinger. Wasting no time, he leaned toward her and kissed her full on the lips.

The kiss heated Lexa's cheeks and Josh smiled. "You're beautiful when you've just been kissed." When her cheeks reddened more, Josh reached for another biscuit. "I have some news for you. I received information about Ted Stanley."

"What did you find out?"

Josh ate half the biscuit and swallowed. "It's what we 'n't find out."

She was puzzled as she tore a Wash 'n Dri packet open to wipe her fingers. "I don't understand."

"Mr. Stanley doesn't exist. He has no social security number or birth certificate. Despite what he told you, he never graduated from Temple." Josh finished his biscuit and brushed the crumbs from his hands into the cardboard bucket.

"I don't believe it. I mean, I don't like him but it's hard to believe he's a total fraud. We've got to tell everyone."

Josh shook his head in warning. "The only thing we can do is tell everybody not to invest or to stop payment on checks. We can't make accusations we can't prove."

"But you said there's no record—"

Josh cut in to explain. "As thorough as Mark is, he says he might have missed something. He thinks this guy is a fraud but there is a corporation on the record for Leisureville."

"So what can we do to prove he's not on the level?"

"Mark suggested we get his fingerprints. If he's a con artist, he's probably done this before and he's using an alias."

"Can't we just give this to the police?"

"Mark says we don't have a case. Believe it or not, Stanley doesn't need special credentials or a license to be a financial advisor. The corporation he's promoting is on the books. It might be a dummy, but we can't prove that yet. There's so much red tape. While Mark does more digging, we could get lucky with the prints. I have to figure out how to get them."

Lexa wiped her fingers with the towelette. "I'll get them."

Josh put the lid on the bucket with a thump. "That's not a good idea. If he's shady and he suspects something, he could be dangerous."

She smiled coyly. "He won't suspect anything."

"Lexa, I don't like the idea of you—"

"It'll be simple. There are so many excuses I can use to see him again. I can tell him I want to add to my portfolio."

"He might think that's strange."

She put the towelette into the bag that had held the

French fries and crumpled it. "No, he won't. Believe me, I can be very convincing."

"And how are you going to get the fingerprints? Steal something from his office?"

"I could invite him over for a drink."

Josh scowled. "No. Don't even think about it." He turned Lexa's chin toward him with a gentle nudge of his knuckle. "Understand?"

She sighed, knowing he was right, knowing she should play it safe. "I'll think of something."

Josh's knuckle slid up her cheek tenderly. "We don't know what we're dealing with. I don't want you involved. I'll find a way to get his prints."

She covered his fingers with her hand and squeezed. "It's easier for me. You might make him suspicious if you ask questions. What if he skips town with everybody's money?"

The beat of the sleet on the truck's roof was the only sound until Josh said, "Okay. Try to get the prints. But do not under any circumstances take a chance. Agreed?"

"Is that an order, Sergeant?"

He grinned. "You bet. And I won't tolerate insubordination."

"I'll be careful," she promised.

Josh inclined toward her, but the chicken bucket was an obstacle between them. He trailed his finger along her neck to the vee of her sweatshirt. "Let's go home." The element of husky promise in his voice made excitement skip up her spine.

Josh packed the refuse from their lunch into the bucket. He was anxious to get Lexa to his dry and warm apartment to finish the conversation they had started. Maybe with a couple of glasses of wine, some soft music, a cuddling atmosphere, she'd let her guard down and tell him exactly how she felt about him.

After they fastened their seat belts, Josh started the truck and switched on the windshield wipers, but the sleet froze on the windshield and visibility was poor.

Josh drove carefully, well under the speed limit. The pinged against the hood and coated the road in the evening dusk. The grinding swish of the windshield wipers did little to clear the glass. Lexa found her hands clenched into fists at her sides and she consciously released them, taking a deep breath to relax. Josh's hands were competently guiding the wheel but the lines around his mouth showed his intense concentration.

The car in front of them spun suddenly in a circle. Josh swore, sharply turned the wheel, and pumped the brakes. His truck spun around and lurched onto the soft shoulder of the road, angling unevenly. Lexa's arm and shoulder had bumped into the door, but her seat belt kept her from flying forward.

She was trying to get her bearings when Josh's hand capped her knee. "Lexa, are you all right?"

Before she could get any words out, he had switched on the inside light. "Lexa, are you okay?"

She turned toward him. "I think so. How about you?" She saw a red spot on his forehead beginning to discolor. "Josh, you hit your head. Let me see."

He brushed her hand away. "I'm fine. We should get out and make sure everything's working, but we'd be inviting pneumonia. Are you sure you're okay?"

"Yes, just shaky. What about the other car?"

"He's gone. Since there was no collision, I guess he felt there was no need to stop." Josh unsnapped his seat belt and moved toward Lexa, putting his arm around her. She was trembling. He hugged her as best he could with her seat belt attached. She snuggled into his neck and he held her for a few moments. "I've got to get the truck back on the road. I don't want to cause an accident." He kissed her temple, moved away, and refastened his seat belt.

The truck sputtered twice before it purred to life. Josh switched the heater on high and backed away from a fence post they had almost hit head-on. "It's a good thing no one was behind us," he muttered to himself.

When Josh pulled into Lexa's driveway, they both heaved sighs of relief. After they reached the dry warmth of Lexa's living room, Josh took her in his arms and held her close. Leaning back, he took her face between his hands. "Are you really all right? If anything had happened to you . . ."

She stroked the bruise on his forehead. "I'm fine. But I think you need some ice."

He shook his jacket off, helped her with hers, and pulled her down on the sofa. "What I need is to hold you in my arms."

Lexa snuggled up next to him. "We could light a fire."

"We could. But I don't want to let you go long enough to do it."

His blue gaze was so intense, it scared her. Her feelings for him scared her. When his lips came down on hers in a no-holds-barred kiss, their passion scared her. Their tongues met, detonating the fuse on a chain reaction. Josh's passion burned through Lexa's blood, passion that threatened to burst whenever they touched or kissed. She kneaded his shoulders, glorying in the muscular strength under her fingers. He smelled like rain and wind and a much more basic aroma that was purely male and sensual. She pushed against him, needing more contact, wanting to get as close as she possibly could. He had a hold on her heart, a strong hold that made her want to give more.

Josh's thumbs pressed into Lexa's shoulders as he pushed her back on the sofa and followed her down. Her hair filtered through his fingers as he angled his mouth for greater access. But kissing wasn't enough. To have her in his arms naked, her legs intertwined with his, was a fantasy he had entertained since the day they'd met. Josh couldn't quell the rush of fire to his loins. He leaned toward the inside of the couch so his fingers could unfasten her blouse buttons. He separated the material, unhitched the clasp on her bra, and with shaking fingers cupped her breast in his hand.

He unsealed his lips from hers and cascaded kisses across her chin, down her throat. The urgency in his groin made his voice raspy. "God, Lexa. You're so soft."

His words were a fiery crackle in her ear. She stretched into his hand, craving his touch. His implacable maleness provoked her hands to caress his back, explore his definition as his body pressed fervently into hers.

Josh's desire became uncontrolled, as wild as a hurricane's winds. He wanted more. His pulse throbbed as he tasted one nipple. Lexa gasped and murmured his name. His knee slipped between her legs as his hand danced across her midriff. When she arched up against him, Josh's fingers unsnapped her jeans. His breathing was ragged from wanting her, needing to fill her and make her his. He had thought he could control the hunger she awakened in him, but he couldn't. He rubbed against her so she'd know exactly what she was doing, what he wanted and needed to quench the raging inferno she was inciting.

They would scale the heights of passion together. The first time they made love would be unforgettable, he'd make sure of that. He stroked her cheek with a shaky hand. "Lexa, let me make love to you. Sweetheart, I want to love you."

Lexa's nerves were overloading with sensations until she felt as if she'd explode. How would it feel to have him deep within? She wanted his love. She wanted all of him with a need too encompassing to deny. But not now, not yet.

Lexa closed her eyes, took a breath, and said, "No."

Her answer didn't compute immediately. Apparently Josh had expected her to say "yes."

"I'm not ready." She could barely choke out the words, but she knew she had to.

"No?" Josh was breathing raggedly. "What are you afraid of?"

Him, the passion between them, the future. "I'm just not ready, Josh." She wriggled, attempting to pull out from under him.

"Lexa, stay still. I need a minute or two."

Lexa went still, afraid to breathe, afraid she'd make the situation even more awkward than it was. When Josh shoved himself up and sat on the edge of the sofa, his head in his hands, she managed, "Josh, I'm sorry."

His gaze sharpened as he gained control. Unspent passion gave a hard edge to his voice when he raised his head. "I don't want you to be sorry. I want to know what's wrong. You want this as much as I do. Why won't you let it happen?"

She lowered her eyes, refastened her bra with fumbling

fingers, and began buttoning her blouse. "I can't. Not yet."

Josh's angry frustration exploded. "Dammit, Lexa, why not?"

"Don't be angry."

He ravaged her with his eyes. "I'm not angry! I'm frustrated with taking it nice and sweet and slow. We're adults and we should both know what we want. I know what I want. Do you?"

Her brown eyes pleaded with him to understand. "It's too soon."

Now he *was* angry and he couldn't keep it from showing. "Do you even know what you feel? Do you want to feel love? Or is it that you have so much compassion to give everyone else you have no feelings left for me? Is that it?"

She dropped her eyes to her lap. "No, that's not it. Of course I have feelings for you."

"Then tell me what they are!"

Lexa fell silent, thinking. No children. She couldn't have children. Why wouldn't the words come out? She felt her emotions welling up, coming much too close to the surface. She was tired and still shaky from their near accident. "Josh, I think you'd better go."

His gaze locked to hers. "If I go, we can't talk; we can't solve any problems."

"I need some time." The rigidity of his posture scared her. "Josh, please try to understand."

He crossed to her and looked down. "I don't understand. I want a relationship. I'm not sure we're any nearer to that now than the first day we met. How are we going to get close if you won't share your time or your passion with me? You'd better decide if you want to put as much energy into your own life as you put into everyone else's." He grabbed his coat and dived into it as if it were the enemy.

Anger still furrowed on his brow as he gave her a last hard look and left without a goodbye. It wasn't until she heard the motor start that Lexa remembered her bicycle was still in his truck.

Chapter Six

Lexa told herself it was better this way. Yes, she'd fallen in love with Josh. But her life had too many complications for a man to accept. Josh had proven that, hadn't he? Damn it, she had to stop thinking about Josh. The best way to do that was to do something else, like going to see Ted Stanley.

But how could she get his fingerprints? Looking for ideas, she took her scarf out of her purse and dumped the rest of its contents onto the desk. Half a minute later, she smiled.

Half an hour later, she hoped that smile was innocent and relaxed as she looked across Ted Stanley's desk. Even if he wasn't trying to swindle his clients, she didn't like him. He was too slick; his answers came too easily. When she had called for an appointment, he had been obliging, saying he could fit her in right away. He was now explaining exactly what he could do with the sum in her savings account.

As if considering his suggestions seriously, she said, "Those stocks sound risky with economic conditions being what they are. You know, the trade deficit and all that."

Ted Stanley's eyes narrowed as if considering Lexa in a

new light. "I must commend you, Ms. Kittredge. You know more about finances than any woman I've ever met."

She let her lashes flutter down demurely. "Thank you, Mr. Stanley. I read a lot."

He eyed her legs as she crossed them. "I'm not sure you need a financial planner. You seem to know what you want."

She had to be careful. He was beginning to get suspicious. "I don't know everything, and I've always believed two heads are better than one."

"Usually," he replied succinctly, letting his eyes slide again from her head to her toes.

She didn't like his bold stares but it wouldn't be wise to alienate him. Not until she got what she came for. "I know I'm probably being silly, but being a single woman, I feel I have to prepare for my future. I thought maybe you could give me some hints about IRAs or annuities and which give the highest interest."

After he had explained two and not mentioned Leisureville, she said, "A few of the senior citizens were telling me about investments in a retirement community."

His almost black eyes narrowed and he looked at her warily. His answer was suave. "That's a shorter-term investment. Five to ten years. If you're planning for your retirement, you need something longer with more equity."

"I see." It was time to end the meeting before she sank in deeper than she could handle. As she stood, she concluded, "I'll certainly think about everything you've explained." When she reached across his desk and extended her hand, she accidentally dropped her purse and its contents spilled out.

"Oh, I'm sorry!" She reached for her wallet and stuffed it in. "You know what they say about women carrying everything but the kitchen sink."

Stanley picked up a mirror and a lipstick and was going to hand them to her, but she opened her purse wide to let him drop them inside. She extended her hand again and shook his. "Thanks again. I'll get back to you when I decide what I want to do." After a nod and a goodbye, she left his office.

Once outside, she heaved a sigh of relief. She had his fingerprints. Now all she had to do was send them to Josh's friend.

Lunch held no appeal as she sat at her desk again, trying not to think about Josh, but not doing a very good job of it. She'd pushed a stack of papers from the left side of the desk to the right when her secretary came in and laid a package on her blotter.

When Joanne went back to her office, Lexa tore off the white bow and unwrapped the bright blue paper, lifting the lid on the box, wondering who could have sent it.

She pulled the tissue back carefully and blinked her eyes. It was a stuffed doll about twelve inches high, with scraggly bright red hair that stood out like a wild halo. The doll's black eyes were crossed, the mouth drawn in a pout. Lexa picked up the note that was tucked into the doll's overalls.

> Lexa, did I look like this last night? I'm sorry about the temper tantrum. I want to make love to you, but only when you're ready. Can we talk?
> Love, Josh

Tears misted in Lexa's eyes as she reached for the phone and dialed The Toy Tank. She gave her name to the person who answered, asked for Josh, and waited without thinking about what she was going to say. "Love, Josh." Could he mean that?

"Lexa?" Josh's deep baritone rumbled through the wire.

"Hi, Josh. I got the package," she said softly.

"Well, does he look like me?"

She laughed. "Not quite."

"Whew! I'm glad to hear it. When I got home last night and looked in the mirror, that's what I saw."

"Josh, it wasn't your fault. I should have . . . I'd like to talk to you tonight."

"Where would you like to go?"

"How about my place? I'll make us a late dinner."

"What can I bring?"

"Just yourself."

Lexa settled on a time with Josh and hung up. Now all she had to do was get through the rest of the day, make dinner, and figure out exactly how she was going to tell Josh what she had to tell him.

Josh gave himself a talking-to as he walked up to Lexa's front door. He was experienced enough to know that sex was no good without love and trust. When a man and a woman made love, they were both at their most vulnerable physically and emotionally. Naked bodies released naked emotions. Was Lexa afraid to have her emotions released? Was she afraid he wouldn't love Dani's child? Or did she simply need more time to decide?

He rang Lexa's doorbell deciding he wasn't going to throw away what he and Lexa were building. He was going to be a gentleman, a perfect gentleman. If it killed him.

When Lexa opened the door, she looked as vulnerable as he'd ever seen her. Her eyes were wide with a questioning anxiety that cut him to the quick.

He didn't want her to be afraid, certainly not of him or what he felt for her.

She led him inside. "Supper will be ready in a little while. I . . ."

"Lexa?"

She turned and faced him. He approached her slowly. "I'm sorry. I don't want to pressure you. I know you have a lot on your mind, especially the baby."

She smiled then, so sweetly his heart practically turned over. "I want us to spend more time together. But I don't know how much my life's going to change. I'm not sure what I should cut out, what I should keep."

He stroked her cheek. "Let me be a part of the changes."

Tears came to her eyes and there was no way he could keep from taking her in his arms. He tried to be gentle and easy, but Lexa's response drove gentle and easy from his mind. The kiss became forceful, his tongue demanding, telling her how much he wanted her. She answered the demand with demands of her own. Her hands roamed his back restlessly, seeking more intimacy. She arched against him, meeting the thrust of his desire. He was almost gone.

He pulled away and dragged in some air. "Lexa, I said I don't want to push you, but if we keep this up—"

Lexa heard what he was saying and she knew she should tell him she couldn't have children. But she loved being in his arms, she loved drowning in his kisses, she needed to be loved. She couldn't give up this one precious time she might never have again. She'd never felt this way about a man and she was afraid she'd lose him.

Couldn't she have this one night?

"I want you to make love to me, Josh. I want to make love to you."

"You're sure?"

She nodded.

Josh searched her eyes for a long moment, then swept her into his arms and carried her upstairs.

When he set her down next to the bed, he couldn't bear to let her go. He wrapped her in his arms and ran his hand down the back of her head. He felt protective—so protective.

Lexa leaned back and braced her hands on his chest. His heart began thumping faster. "Do you see what you do to me?" he asked.

She reached for the hem of his shirt and lifted it over his head. He helped her and dropped it on the floor. When she ran her hands across his chest, down to his waistband, he shuddered. And when she said, "You do the same thing to me," he reached for the hem of her sweater.

After pulling it over her head, he combed her hair into place with his fingers. "I love your hair. It's so soft and so natural." His hands cruised down her arms and back up. He unhooked her bra and stared. "Your skin's so white, so delicate. You're as beautiful on the outside as you are on the inside, Lexa. I want to touch you and know every part of you."

Her eyes were wider and darker than he'd ever seen them. "I'm going to please you, Josh. I want to give you what you want."

"You will, sweetheart. You will."

Josh's body stirred. She was so sensual and unafraid of her sexuality or his. That in itself was a potent turn-on.

After they had undressed each other, Josh threw the covers back and lay down next to Lexa. He slid his fingers under her hair while his thumbs caressed her neck. Softly, like the spring rain kissing the earth, he showered small kisses over her face.

Lexa was surrounded by Josh's heat, his clean maleness, the blue smoke in his eyes, the cosmic wonder of being in love. There was no past, no future, only now. When he nudged her head toward his, she reached for him, lost in his sensual drugging. She could never be immune to him. His breath kissed her cheek an instant before his lips—warm, demanding, sharing—rested on hers. His tongue flicked across their surface, patiently waiting for her to give him entrance.

Josh couldn't hold back as his body surged toward Lexa's. His hands seemed to be designed for the curves of her body as his tongue explored the sweet recesses of her mouth. Sparks ricocheted in all directions and pricked through every part of him.

Lexa linked her arms around Josh as he deepened the kiss. Her heart skipped too many beats to count and heat burned between her thighs. Reality exploded into another dimension where there was love, sensation, union. Lexa's tongue met Josh's with unchecked hunger and she drew him down on top of her. While his mouth plundered and seduced, his hands slid up her leg until he encountered her navel. His thumb drew circles around it, teasing her, testing her, inciting a firestorm of electricity.

Sliding her hand up his hip, Lexa felt his shiver as if it were hers. When he moved suggestively, she became bolder, moving her hand between his thighs in search of his manhood.

Josh shifted to his side and nudged her until she faced him. His lips left hers and cascaded kisses over her cheeks down her neck to her shoulder. His hand wandered to the nest of golden hair to test her readiness. He taunted until a moan erupted from her throat. He asked raspily, "Do you want me as much as I want you?"

"Yes," she responded breathlessly as her hand enclosed him.

He stared at her, binding her to him with his eyes. "I have never wanted a woman the way I want you."

"You're an incredibly sexy man."

"I need you, Lexa."

"Show me how much," she whispered.

His eyes darkened in the mellow glow of the lamp. "I want to prolong this."

"That doesn't matter, Josh. Just love me and let me love you."

His fingers quested up and down her back until he wove them through her hair and pressed her head toward his. Kissing her was such a sensual experience. Her kisses lasted, stayed with him, for him to savor when she wasn't near. Her lips were already parted and inviting. He accepted the invitation.

The tiny pulse at Lexa's throat fluttered. Josh's lips kissed down her throat to her breast. When he took the hardened rosy tip into his mouth and rolled it around on his tongue, she felt like a tornado looking for a place to spin. Her hands searched through his thick black hair to his scalp and massaged in a rhythmic pattern in keeping with his mouth as he owned the crest of her breast.

When his tongue flicked out, circling the peak, she arched upward, offering him more. "Oh, Josh. That feels so good."

Lexa needed to show Josh she loved him, to incite in him the same feelings he was inciting in her. She'd decided to take tonight, each precious moment, and live it to its fullest. Because she didn't know what would come after tonight, what would come after he knew . . .

She blanked out thoughts of the future and pushed on his shoulder until he received her message and lay back. Each of her movements was measured and provocative as she curled on her side next to him. Her knee rubbed his hair-roughened thigh as her fingers sketched playful designs on his chest. She pecked at his shoulder, stopped to gently tug at a nipple, and nipped at his tight abdomen with her teeth. Her hands were busy fondling and stroking the velvet landscape that was the most tender.

"Sweetheart," he rasped. "I can't hold on much longer." She raised her head and, with a graceful movement, straddled his legs. His hands spanned her slim waist then guided her hips until their bodies fused.

The heart of Lexa's womanhood tensed, relaxed, tensed again until neither of them could control the fire that was consuming them both. Lexa gloried in each nuance of contact as she watched Josh's eyes. She let him set the rhythm, knowing she could explode at any moment. She moved in counterpoint against him, allowing him to thrust deeper and deeper until they composed their own symphony of light and motion and sound that climaxed to a mighty crescendo. A shower of shudders rippled through her body as she heard Josh's cry of fulfillment seconds after her own.

Lexa nestled in the crook of Josh's arm feeling more loved than she'd ever felt. He hadn't said the words, nor had she. But the feeling was there.

Josh tightened his arm around Lexa and she turned toward him. He passed his hand over her hip. "I hope that was as wonderful for you as it was for me."

"It was."

Josh's eyes darkened. "How long can I stay?"

She rubbed her hand over his chest. "How long do you want to stay?"

His voice was husky. "All night."

They shared a deeply satisfying kiss. Lexa stroked his chest, and pulled away to look into his eyes.

"Josh, would you like to come home with me for Thanksgiving? I don't want to take you away from Clare, but I'd like you to meet Dani. She's going to tell Dad about the baby."

Josh looked pleased. "I think Clare will understand. She and her housemates are inviting a few friends from the senior center who don't have family nearby." He kissed

Lexa's forehead. "I want to be part of your life. I'd like to go home with you."

"Maybe we can have supper with Clare before we go. But wait . . . I just thought, isn't the Friday after Thanksgiving your busiest day of the year? I was going to stay until Sunday . . ."

"I have competent employees and an excellent manager." He tipped up her chin. "You're more important."

If she hadn't been in love with Josh before, that would have done it. She wrapped her arms around his neck and kissed him from the bottom of her heart.

Lexa headed for a meeting at the senior center, thinking about Josh. She'd told him she'd join him at his apartment after her meeting. Last night had been wonderful, more wonderful than she'd ever dreamed. After the first time they'd made love, Josh had used birth control as a matter of course. She could have said something then, she should have, but everything had been so wonderful, she hadn't wanted to spoil it. So she'd decided she'd tell Josh about her sterility after their trip to her home. Meeting Dani and her father would be enough for now.

Lexa found a seat next to Clare and listened to the agenda for December. She kept checking her watch. Clare nudged her arm. "It's five minutes later than the last time you looked."

She smiled sheepishly. "Am I that obvious?"

"Just to me. Do you have a date with Josh?"

"Um-hmm."

Clare gave her a knowing smile.

Lexa leaned close to Clare and in a low voice asked, "Does your house feel like a home yet?"

Clare's blue eyes sparkled like Josh's. "Sure does. It's so nice to sit in the parlor at night and talk with friends who have the same concerns. We like the same music, we've shared the same historical events, we're in no hurry when we play Scrabble because we've stopped rushing like young people do. It's a comfortable life."

"You sound happy."

"I am. It was the best decision I ever made."

When Lexa looked at her watch again, Clare thumped her on the shoulder. "Get going, Lexa. There's no reason to stick around here when you want to be elsewhere."

"I can't. I have to tell everyone something they won't want to hear."

When the business meeting was over, Lexa was recognized and stood. Heads turned toward her. Her tone was as serious as her expression. "I have reason to believe Mr. Stanley's financial planning might not be the best."

One of the men tapped his cane and called out, "Is he crooked?"

Lexa answered, "I'm not sure yet. But until I can get more information, I don't think you should invest your money."

"What if we already did?" a rotund grandmotherly type asked."

"I think you should stop payment on your checks." At grunts of disapproval and dismay, Lexa offered, "I know that's some trouble and I know Mr. Stanley won't like it, but you've got to protect yourselves. I could be all wrong about this, and I hope I am. If I am, I will personally apologize to Mr. Stanley. But until we discover if he's kosher, your money will be safer in your bank."

"My son-in-law invested money in Leisureville. What should I tell him and my daughter?" Edna Jenkins inquired, her voice shaky.

"How old is your son-in-law, Edna?" Lexa asked.

"Twenty-eight."

That information added more wood to Stanley's pyre. If he had advised Lexa against Leisureville because it wasn't long-term, why would he recommend it to Edna's son-in-law? "Tell them the same thing I told you. If you know anybody else who is going to go to Stanley, tell them to wait until they hear from you."

The crowd began murmuring loudly. Lexa raised her voice to say, "Because of Thanksgiving, I probably won't hear anything until the end of next week. Until then, you can send up some prayers and hope I'm wrong."

As the group continued to mumble and some stood to

disperse, Edna motioned to Lexa. She met the older lady in the middle of the aisle.

Edna said, "I'm scared. I invested five thousand dollars. What if I never see it again? I can't afford to lose it."

Lexa put her hand on Edna's shoulder. "We'll get to the bottom of this as soon as we can. We can't prove anything yet, so we can't make accusations."

"Is that nice Mr. Flannigan helping you? You certainly shouldn't be trying to do this yourself."

Lexa smiled. "Yes, he's helping, and he has a friend who's helping him."

Lexa was anxious to get home. After she tried to reassure Edna again about her investment, she said good night to Clare and left before anyone else could tie her up.

She'd never been this eager to leave a meeting before. She'd never been this eager to see someone. Josh was changing her life. Was she ready for the change?

The Kittredge home was magnificent. A long driveway, tall white pillars on the porch, an affluence of rooms, damasks, Oriental rugs, and Fabergé eggs. Josh wondered about Lexa's childhood, whether she ran through the rooms with pigtails flying, whether she played with toys scattered around the antique spinning wheel, whether she ever did her homework on the polished mahogany dining room table. He doubted it. After a formal introduction to Donald Kittredge, the housekeeper Anna showed them to separate rooms.

After Josh and Lexa unpacked, they walked down the wide open staircase together. Josh grinned. "Are you going to sneak into my room tonight or am I going to sneak into yours?"

"Afraid a monster will get you in a strange bed?"

As they reached the landing, he targeted her ribs and began tickling. "You have no respect."

She tried unsuccessfully to push away his hands but they were too large and too quick. "Stop it. Coercion won't work!"

"Who says?" He started a fresh attack.

She slapped at his hands between giggles. "Josh, Dad's in the living room."

He stopped tickling but kept her a prisoner in his arms. "I'll stop if you give me a nice, long kiss."

"Blackmail," she said but with a pleasurable sigh let him kiss her at length. The magic and excitement was always there, the passion ever-burning. His breath became hers. Hers became his. She pushed away a pang of guilt. She'd tell him she couldn't have children. Soon. But meeting Dani this weekend, seeing the reality of having a baby, was enough to throw at him now.

Josh finally broke off the kiss.

Breathless, she said, "I'll sneak into *your* room. You have the king-size bed." She jabbed him in the ribs, then scurried down the remaining steps into the living room before he could catch her.

When Josh came into the living room and took a seat next to her on the sofa, his look said, "I'll get you later."

Donald Kittredge smiled at the two of them. "I hope Dani isn't too late. Anna says she can't hold dinner much longer; the turkey will fall apart."

"Dani will be here soon." Lexa checked her watch.

"She'll be here when she's good and ready," her father disagreed, his brown eyes saying he knew better.

"Dad, you have to have faith in her."

Donald adjusted his wire rims. "You don't see Dani's flaws like I do."

Her father had always been harder on Dani than his older daughter, maybe because Lexa had always tried to be the perfect daughter while Dani rebelled. Sometimes she wondered if he loved either of them. He'd missed important events in their lives. Birthday parties. Dani's graduation from eighth grade. The ceremony when Lexa had received the American Legion medal for good citizenship. She tried to forget the Thanksgiving dinners planned by her stepmother to include the "right" people, people who raised her to upper-echelon society.

"Did Anna tell you I bought her a new oven? It's hard to believe she's been with us twenty-eight years. We hired her when we bought this house." This he directed to Josh.

Josh said, "Loyalty and staying power are important in the people who work for you."

"Loyalty has a great deal to do with the amount of their paycheck."

"Dad."

"Lexa, that's just the way it is."

Was he really that cynical? How was he going to respond when he knew Dani was pregnant, when he knew Lexa was adopting the baby? Josh covered Lexa's hand with his and she was glad he was here.

Donald turned to Josh. "Lexa told me you own two toy stores. I respect a man who manages his finances well enough to enable growth."

"Dad, it's Thanksgiving. Can we keep business out of the conversation?" Lexa asked quietly.

Her father shrugged and ran his fingers through his thinning brown hair. "We can try." After a brief silence, Donald asked Josh, "How long have you and Lexa been dating?"

"About six weeks," Josh said.

"Lexa doesn't tell me much when she calls. She gives me the time she's arriving, the time she's departing."

"You make me sound like a jet."

"You move like one most of the time," her father grumbled. "The only time you're still is when you're hashing out some plot with Dani."

Suddenly from the doorway, a voice interrupted. "Hi, everyone. I'm not late for dinner, am I?"

Lexa motioned to Dani to come to the sofa. "No. You're just in time. Come meet Josh."

Dani approached the sofa. Her eyes swept Josh's figure and his face. She grinned and said in a mock aside to Lexa, "You picked a winner this time."

Lexa tried to keep a blush from coloring her cheeks. She hugged Dani. "We didn't hear you come in."

Dani brushed her sister's words away with her hand. "I came in the back." After the hug, she extended her hand to Josh. "Lexa's told me what a great guy you are. She sure was right about your gorgeous blue eyes." Lexa wanted to sink under the sofa.

Josh winked and squeezed her knee.

Dani rubbed her hands on the oversize shirt that fell over faded denims. She cast a worried glance at her father. "I think we should just get this over with right away, Lexa. Don't you?"

Lexa's stomach jumped. "Why don't you wait until after dinner?"

"Get what over with?" Donald asked.

"Dad, I'm pregnant. Rob doesn't want to get married. I'm going to have the baby and Lexa's going to adopt him or her. Lexa and I have talked about this until we're blue. It's settled." Dani stuffed her hands in her pockets after the rushed recital.

Donald Kittredge's mouth dropped open and he sat in stunned silence looking at Dani and then Lexa. He closed his mouth and rose to his feet. "Dani, I want to see you in my office. Now."

"Dad . . ."

"Danielle," he repeated in a brook-no-argument voice.

Lexa started to jump to Dani's defense. "Dad—"

Donald turned to his elder daughter, "I want to talk to Dani privately; I'll talk with you after dinner. I'm sure we'll all be discussing this together in the months to come." He motioned Dani out of the room and she followed.

Lexa stood to go in the same direction but Josh caught her arm to stop her. "Let them talk."

"But Josh, I know how he can be. I don't want him upsetting her."

"Do you fight all her battles?"

"No, of course not. But—"

"He's her father," Josh said gently. "He's going to want to know more than the little bit Dani just told him."

"He's so hard to talk to."

"This is his grandchild."

"And he'll have no more time for him or her than he had for us." She felt more sadness than bitterness.

"You don't know that."

"If Dad wants to be a part of my life and a grandfather to the baby, I'll let him. But I don't expect that to happen." She looked again toward the doorway.

Josh cupped her elbow. "Give them some time alone."

She thought about it. "All right. Dani won't let Dad corner her for long." Lexa smiled. "How would you like to carve the turkey?"

Josh let her change the subject. "Will your housekeeper let me? Clare pushes me out of the kitchen when she's cooking."

"Just flash Anna one of your charming smiles and she'll melt in her oxfords."

"And bat my gorgeous blue eyes?" he teased.

"Do you remember *everything*?"

His grin was mischievous. "My brain works like a computer. Every tidbit of information is kept in its memory bank."

Lexa playfully pushed on his shoulder and turned him around. "Into the kitchen, R2D2. We'll find some use for you."

He spun around, swung her into his arms, bent her back, and kissed her thoroughly. When he brought her back up, he asked smugly, "Do you know any other computers that can do that?"

"Not a one," she said breathlessly, grateful he was a man, a very sexy man. The man she loved.

Josh watched the Kittredge family as they ate a superbly prepared Thanksgiving dinner. The atmosphere was tense when Donald Kittredge and Dani returned from their pow-wow and sat at the table. Josh felt uncomfortable when neither of them mentioned their conversation. Worried vibrations were coming from Lexa and he didn't know how to reassure her. Josh did his best to keep the conversation flowing. To his relief, Dani began chattering and joking. Her ebullience clouded the concerns for the moment and the tension relaxed.

Many of her gestures and mannerisms were the same as Lexa's. But there the resemblance stopped. Her hair was dark brown, her eyes hazel. She liked attention. So different from Lexa.

As Lexa relaxed and began eating, Josh watched her act as a buffer between Dani and her father. Josh was sitting next to Donald, and while Dani and Lexa discussed common friends and Christmas presents for relatives, Lexa's father quizzed Josh about his educational background and his family.

After Anna had served pumpkin pie, Lexa saw what was happening and gave Josh an encouraging smile. He smiled back.

Donald Kittredge saw the exchange. "Josh, I have some interesting puzzles in the den that I've collected over the years. Would you like to see them?"

"I thought you wanted to talk to me," Lexa said.

"We have until Saturday. This problem isn't going to go away. I'd like to get to know Josh better. How about it, Josh? Can we retire to my office?"

Josh wanted to get to know this man. By understanding Donald Kittredge, he could better understand Lexa. "Sure." He stood and pushed his chair back. The look he gave Lexa said, "Don't worry."

Dani poked her sister. "We can go bother Anna."

"We can help Anna," Lexa corrected, a wary eye on her father as the two men departed.

Donald Kittredge's office smelled of wood and leather. Shelves lined two walls, an immense mahogany desk was set against one wall, and two burgundy leather chairs with ottomans faced a red brick fireplace.

After Josh had examined the shelves and the puzzles shaped like a cube, a chocolate kiss, and a ball within a square, Donald invited him to sit in front of the fireplace. He began with a pointed question. "Are you and Lexa seriously involved?"

"Yes, we are."

"Do you believe Lexa knows what she's doing in adopting this child?"

"With due respect, Mr. Kittredge, I think you should ask Lexa that."

Donald Kittredge's brows drew together. "Lexa and I have trouble talking to each other. She gets very defensive, especially where Dani is concerned."

"From what Lexa has told me, that seems only natural."

He acknowledged the observation with a nod. "She's

probably told you more than she's told me. First of all,
I'm worried about both of them. This situation is sticky,
very sticky. Lexa always knows her own mind; Dani doesn't.
My younger daughter tends to be impulsive and likes to
take the easy way out.''

"It's not easy to carry a child to term and then give it
up," Josh offered. "She's made a mature decision wanting
to put the child's welfare first."

"Maybe. Personally, I think she would like nothing better than to marry Rob and settle down. That's not possible
so she's going to have the child, let Lexa have custody, yet
she can be Aunt Dani and enjoy playing with the baby,
visiting when she wants."

Josh had been so caught up in Lexa's excitement about
the child that he hadn't thought about the complications.
"Lexa feels the child will be hers. She'll be the mother,
not Dani."

"Legally perhaps. But we can't legalize our emotions. I
feel Dani should keep the baby. I'll give her whatever
assistance she needs. You and Lexa need a solid relationship before you consider having children or adopting
them. Dani's due in May. That doesn't give you and Lexa
much time together alone."

Josh bristled at Donald Kittredge's assessment of what
he and Lexa needed, but for Lexa's sake and his own, he
kept his temper in check. He *was* worried about the limited
time they had together. Lexa was so involved. With a child,
she would be even more involved. Would she have time
for him and their relationship? As much to himself as to
Donald Kittredge, he said, "We can work it out."

"You seem to be supportive of Lexa. But consider what
I've said. She thinks she can save the world, but I'm not
sure this is the time to save Dani. If Dani was forced to
give this child up to a stranger, she wouldn't. She'd keep
it."

"You don't know that, Dad. You don't know that at all."

Donald looked over the back of his chair when he heard
Lexa's voice. "Lexa, I don't think you've given this enough
thought."

She came into the room and stood in front of the two

men. "I've given this days and weeks of thought. This decision is right and I don't want you trying to talk Dani out of it. Let us solve this ourselves."

Donald Kittredge's voice was firm, his eyes penetrating. "You're not solving it correctly. What happens if in a year or two Dani grows up and decides she wants the child back? Then what are you going to do?"

"That won't happen," Lexa denied.

Josh asked gently, "But what if it does?"

"You're not taking his side, are you?"

"I'm not taking anybody's side, but you'd better look at this from all the angles." Josh knew Lexa would be devastated if she gave all her love and then Dani wrenched the child away. Would she let Dani take the baby back? Everything he knew about Lexa told him she wouldn't think of herself first.

"I have looked at this from all angles and that won't happen. You don't know Dani as I do. She'd never do that to me or the baby."

Donald cut in. "I hope not. I sincerely hope she'd consider the welfare of her child rather than her own. But with Dani, it's hard to tell."

Lexa gave a resigned sigh. "You don't know her, and you don't know me. You never took the time." Childhood hurts hadn't healed, might never heal. All Lexa could do was go on from this moment.

A pained look crossed her father's face. "Let's not get into that now. What I'm telling you makes sense from an impartial observer's viewpoint. You think you can solve the world's problems. You think you can give and give and give more, and everything will change. And you think you can do it all by yourself. You can't, Lexa. You simply can't."

"I *can* do it myself. After Mom died, I never had anyone to depend on. Not you. Certainly not Loretta. I've done fine without anybody's help." She had had no choice. That hurt more than she ever wanted to admit.

Her father looked at her for a long moment, turned on his heel, and left the room.

Chapter Seven

Josh spoke first. "What's between you and your dad?"

Lexa sighed, the hurt from years gone by still real and alive. "I don't want to explain it. You'll probably just take his side."

Josh studied her for a moment. "What's really at the bottom of this, Lexa?"

A weariness settled over her. "He doesn't love me. He never did. If I wanted his attention, I had to get it by being outstanding. I had to get the top grades in my class, win the swim meet, earn the blue ribbon. And then if I got anything, it was a pat on the head, his attention for five minutes. That was all. He's got no right to tell me how to run my life now," she ended, her voice vibrating with emotion.

"Your father has a right to worry about you and Dani, even if you don't want to listen to him. What *are* you going to do if you adopt Dani's baby and next year or the year after, she wants it back? If there's any indication that she wants to keep this baby, you should encourage her."

Lexa knew her judgment was shadowed by the past, and Josh was trying to make her see the reality of the situation now. "I have encouraged her. We've weighed the pros and cons. She doesn't want the baby; she wants to get on with her life. Dad has no business trying to persuade her to keep it. I don't want him interfering.''

Josh's blue eyes shone with concern. "Lexa, he wants to advise you. Just listen to him. Don't you want to get closer to him, not only for your sake, but for Dani's and the baby's?''

"Of course I do. But it's not that simple. You're a stranger to the whole thing—''

"Yes, I am. And because I am, I can be more objective than you can. Maybe you should take a long look at the whole situation and try to gain some objectivity yourself.''

Josh stood, gave her a look filled with meaning, and left her alone.

Lexa walked through the backyard, down the flagstone path that led to the rose garden. Rows of bushes formed a square around a bronze sundial. Bare stems with thorns reached toward the gray sky. It was hard to believe that in the spring and summer the garden raged with color. Lexa raised her face to the sky and felt dampness on her face. Rain or sleet was coming. She could sense it, smell it, feel it.

She didn't notice the November bleakness when Josh was around. He was a tonic filling her life with laughter and sunshine. So why couldn't she listen to his advice? He had been blind to his aunt's concerns. Was she blind to her father's? Wasn't it time to make peace or at least attempt to?

Lexa walked the grounds. A fine mist began to fall. When her fingers grew frosty, she stuffed her hands into the pockets of her car coat. Walking by a rock garden that in the warm months housed a three-tiered fountain, she remembered playing in it with Dani.

Did Josh really believe Dani should keep her child? If he did, did that mean he didn't want an adopted child? A man could love children, all children, but still want his own. Where did that leave her?

Lexa's toes became as cold as her nose, and she slowly walked back to the house. She let herself in the sliding glass doors that led into a large family room. Dani was curled on the sofa watching television. She turned down the sound with the remote. "Did you and Dad have a fight?"

"I guess you could say that."

"He means well."

"Maybe he does," Lexa admitted. She studied her sister carefully. "Dani, are you having second thoughts about the adoption, because if you are . . ."

"I'm not, Lexa. I think Dad would like nothing better than to have me move in here with the baby. Don't ask me why, it's just the impression I get. But that's not what I want."

"What do you want?"

"What I want, I can't have."

Fear washed over Lexa. What if Dani and Rob did get back together? How would Josh feel if she didn't adopt this child and then he discovered she couldn't have children? Dani was the only person who knew that.

Lexa sat down next to Dani and hugged her. "I love you. I want you to be happy."

"I know you do, and I will be. Someday." Releasing her sister, Lexa asked, "Where is everybody?"

"Dad's in his office. Josh is in the kitchen raiding the refrigerator. He's really a great guy, sis. You're lucky. Does he know . . . ?"

"That I can't have children? Not yet. I have to tell him . . . soon. Everything's happened so fast." Lexa pushed herself to her feet. "I'm going to talk to Dad. Maybe I can convince him we know what we're doing. We do know what we're doing, don't we?"

Dani's eyes were a bit brighter than usual, but she nodded her head. "Yes. I don't want to give the baby to a stranger. There's no other way."

Lexa patted Dani's hand and went to her dad's office.

Josh felt as if he'd been socked in the eye with a baseball. Stunned. Hurt. And angry as hell. Why hadn't Lexa told him?

He went back to the kitchen, trying to absorb what he'd heard in the hallway. Lexa couldn't have children. That explained a lot. Her defensive attitude about adopting Dani's baby. Her fervor. But most of all, her attitude where their relationship was concerned. He'd known she was being hesitant about something. Lexa was an all-out type of person. But he could sense she was still holding back. And now he knew why.

She couldn't have children. What did that mean to him? To them?

He examined his heart. Yes, he wanted children. But Lexa was more important. He wanted her. They could adopt children. If not Dani's, others. What concerned him most was Lexa's lack of trust.

Had he given her reason *not* to trust him?

When they'd made love, he'd thought they'd opened their hearts to each other. He'd opened his heart to her. She'd kept up a barrier.

Should he confront her or let her come to him?

Donald Kittredge was sitting at his desk, charts lying on the blotter in front of him. He looked up when Lexa sat down in the Windsor chair across from him. "Is it cold enough to snow?"

"Maybe." She rubbed her hands together because they still weren't warm.

Donald's dark brown eyes stared into his daughter's. "Lexa, how can we have a normal father-daughter relationship?"

Her voice cracked when she answered, "I'm not sure what that is."

"Do you have too much resentment built up to try?"

"Dad, I don't know what to say."

"Then don't say anything. Listen."

She nodded.

He steepled his fingers together on the edge of the desk. "I know I wasn't around much when your mother was alive. When you were born, my business was just starting out. I worked eighteen-hour days to give my family everything I could, everything my father couldn't afford to give me. I wanted to send you to the finest schools, buy you the best money could buy. Is there something wrong with that?''

She felt vaguely ashamed. "No, I suppose not. But don't you realize I would have rather had your time instead of a higher income bracket?''

"Honey, I was driven. My father was unemployed during the Depression. Sometimes we didn't have enough food to eat. I swore that would never happen to my family.''

"I never knew that," Lexa said with a glimmer of understanding.

He picked up a sterling letter opener and tapped it on the ball of his thumb. "It wasn't something I liked to talk about. It was a miserable time, better forgotten. But I want you to understand.''

"I understand how it might have started. But did you have to work that hard year after year?''

"I thought I did." He put the swordlike object along the side of the blotter. "Your mother understood me. She understood my need for security—to make enough money so we'd never have to worry about finances, so we could give you and Dani good lives.''

"Money doesn't do that, Dad.''

He leaned forward to try to explain. "I know. I know now. I married Loretta so you'd have more than money.''

"You aren't serious!''

"I am. You were twelve; Dani was eight. You needed a mother.''

"Loretta wasn't a mother. She didn't even care!''

"I didn't see that until too late. I was in so much pain from your mother's death that Loretta seemed like a godsend. It took me too long to find out she wasn't.''

"Five years," Lexa murmured.

Her father sat back with a sigh. "Your mother and I fell in love instantly when we were young. We had immediate trust, immediate respect. I was so anxious to find that again that I let Loretta pull the wool over my eyes. When I woke up and realized what was going on, you and Dani had grown away from me.''

"What finally made you get a divorce? I never knew. It happened so suddenly. One day she was here, the next she was gone."

"She was having an affair. When I confronted her, she admitted it wasn't the first. I ordered her out of the house."

"Dad, I didn't know." Tears came to her eyes for her father, for the hurt he must have felt, the complete sense of betrayal. "How could she do that to you? Why didn't you tell me? Maybe I could have helped."

He smiled. "That's like you, wanting to help. Maybe I should have told you. Maybe it could have brought us back together. You and Dani were practically grown. You were more reserved than Dani. We had no basis for a relationship. I didn't want to spoil your idealism. But maybe I should have told you. Maybe things would be different now if I had." He paused, cleared his throat, and said, "I want you to know, Lexa, I'm proud of you. I'm proud of the way you've looked out for your sister. You might think I didn't notice, but I did. It's why I'm concerned now."

Emotions clogged Lexa's throat. But she finally got out, "Dad, you don't have to be."

"Lexa, let me help."

She swallowed the lump in her throat. "There's nothing to help with. Dani is sure about this and so am I."

"Why are you so sure, honey? You're almost desperate about this."

Maybe if she told him, he'd understand. Maybe it would help her prepare to tell Josh. "Dad, I might never be able to have children."

Her father looked stunned. "You're sure?"

"I've had some testing. The outlook isn't good. I'd love Dani's baby as if it were my own."

"Lexa, I'm so sorry. I know you'd love Dani's baby but . . ." He stopped. "I can see you're determined about this. Dani seems to be too. But will you promise me something?"

"What?"

"If you need help, you'll call me."

This was the olive branch, the starting-over point. Their father wanted to share their lives. Lexa blinked back tears as her heart warmed with a glow that hadn't been there in years. "I'll call you. Or Dani will call you. But don't worry about it, Dad. We'll be all right."

"You can call even if you don't need me. Visit more. I want to spend time with my grandchild, Lexa. Will you let me?"

Compassion for her father, the losses he had sustained—her mother, Loretta—all the pain, the distance between them that was her fault too, overwhelmed Lexa. "Oh, Dad." She smiled tremulously. "Of course I will, if that's what you want. A child can't be loved too much." She watched his eyes glisten with feeling and she realized she had just given her father a gift as well as giving herself one.

"Honey, I've always done what I think is best for you. Maybe that never came through, but it was what I intended."

With sudden insight, Lexa understood one aspect of parenting. "I guess all a parent can do is try his best."

"Do you forgive me for not being around much when you were growing up?"

"I should have tried to understand you better a long time ago."

"I should have tried harder to bridge the gap between us."

They sat quietly for a few minutes until Donald said, "I like Josh."

Lexa said simply, "I do, too." And then she did something she hadn't done in years. She got out of her chair, went around the desk, and gave her father a hug. He hugged her back.

A few minutes later, Lexa found Josh at the breakfast bar in the kitchen with a wedge of pie and a cup of coffee. She went to the coffee maker and poured herself a cup. "It's cold outside." When Josh didn't comment and she glanced at his set expression, she realized there was a chill in here. Was he angry about their almost-argument? She opened the refrigerator, grabbed the carton of milk, and poured some into her coffee.

Carrying the mug to the bar, she hopped up onto the

rattan stool next to Josh. "Did you find what you wanted? There's leftover turkey and stuffing."

He swallowed his last bite of pie and pushed the dish away. "I wasn't that hungry. Dani seemed to want some time alone, so I came in here."

"That was thoughtful."

He shot her a speaking glance. Lexa put her mug down on the counter. "Josh, I'm sorry about earlier. I know you were only trying to help."

"But you can't accept help, can you, Lexa?"

There was an odd note in his voice. She had thought she'd tell him about the conversation with her father and he'd be happy for her. "What do you mean?"

He swung his long body around toward her, one hand braced on the bar, his other set stubbornly on his thigh. "I mean, you know how to give, but you don't know how to receive. You're so damn independent, you can't let anyone help *you*. Let me tell you, Lexa. Giving without receiving is pure manipulation."

"That's not true!" She was hurt that he could feel that way about her.

"It *is* true. If you give and don't accept back, you make others beholden to you. Did you ever think that maybe Dani feels as if she owes you this child?"

"That's ridiculous!"

"No, it's not. You practically raised her."

Lexa buried any doubts she had and defended them both. "She's as sure about this as I am."

"Are you trying to earn Dani's approval? Or your father's?"

"I'm not trying to get anyone's approval."

"I'm not so sure about that. You do it all the time. You make a career of serving others to get their approval."

Anger rose in her but she kept a lid on it. "You're wrong."

"I don't think so. You admitted you wanted your dad's attention and approval when you were growing up. And you never felt as if you earned it. So you give and do for everyone you can, to get the pat on the back you never received. I think you're afraid to let yourself be loved for who you are rather than what you do."

"I think your amateur analysis is off the wall! *I'm* the one who took psychology in college."

"A lot of good it did if you can't use it for your own benefit."

She turned away from him, picked up her mug, jumped off the stool, and poured her coffee in the sink. She started to leave the kitchen, but as quick as lightning, Josh stood up and grabbed her shoulders. "Don't run away from me."

She tried to twist away. "I see no reason to stay here and let you take pot shots at me." As his hands gripped harder, she ordered, "Let me go."

He held up his hands, freeing her. "Okay, go."

His easy surrender made her stand stock-still. Josh could see the hurt in her eyes. He'd handled this all wrong. He was hurt she couldn't confide in him, and he wondered why. Why didn't she trust him?

He'd wanted her to see she could rely on people, too, that she could confide in him and he'd still love her. But he'd gone about it the wrong way. Even if he was right about the way she'd grown up, he shouldn't have let it all spill out like that—like an accusation. That would only push her farther away. Until she trusted him, she wouldn't confide in him.

The hurt on her face squeezed Josh's heart. He never wanted to hurt her. There was only one thing he could say that might make a difference. He hadn't said it yet, maybe because he sensed she was still resisting him. But maybe if he took the risk of saying it first, she'd understand she could trust him.

"Lexa, I love you."

"Oh, Josh. I . . ."

He put his fingers over her lips. "You don't have to say anything."

Her eyes filled with tears.

He locked his hands behind her back. "Think about what I said, okay? You're a loving, compassionate woman. And you don't have to *do* anything to be loved. I love you just the way you are."

She stroked his jaw. "You're so important to me, Josh. And that makes me afraid."

"Don't be afraid. We'll find our way together. Trust me."

He saw the anxiety and the doubts in her eyes. He didn't know how to wipe them away. So he kissed her. When he began the kiss, he held back—until she parted her lips. He claimed ownership, branded, demanded. His arms brought her against his chest. Her breasts thrust forward, and by the hardening of her nipples, he could tell she was aroused.

He let his kiss tell her how much he loved her. He wanted to draw from her all the love she could give, but he wanted to give to her too . . . and teach her how to receive.

He tore his mouth from hers and nuzzled her neck. "If we don't stop this now, I'll take you on the kitchen table."

She pulled back slowly, and a small smile played across her lips. "That would be a new experience."

He growled, pulled her to him again, and pressed her body into his, beginning at her shoulders, then her back, then her hips. When she shivered from the contact made more delicious by the friction of clothes, he broke the embrace and set her away. "We'd better have a cup of coffee until I have a few minutes to cool down." He leaned his forehead against hers. "I guess you know it's not fair."

"What isn't?"

He drew one finger down the middle of her back over her derriere. "Women can get hot and bothered and nothing shows. It's a little more difficult for a man to hide his feelings."

She smiled at him coyly. "Are you sure you want to hide them?"

"I want to do something about them," he grumbled.

She caressed his cheek with such tenderness, his hand shook. "I'll visit you tonight. After everybody goes to bed."

"You could stay all night."

"Yes, I could."

The doubts were still there. When would she trust him

enough not only to lie in his arms but to tell him she couldn't have children?

When Lexa opened her eyes the next morning, brilliant sun was streaming through the windows. She was turned on her side and Josh's long length was tight against her back, his arm around her waist. She brushed her hair out of her eyes and rubbed her fingers across the forearm that held her captive.

Within a few minutes she felt his lips on the back of her neck. "Mornin'. Did you sleep well?"

She slid on her back within the circle of his arm. "Once I got to sleep," she teased.

His hand spanned her stomach then toured her breast. "Are you complaining?"

"Never." Her body came alive with his touch.

He taunted one pink peak with his forefinger. "I like waking up with you. It could be habit-forming."

She danced her fingers down the middle of his chest. "Habits are hard to break."

"Some don't need to be broken."

She sifted her fingers through his dark chest hair. "There's a habit in this house of having breakfast at eight. Are you up to it?"

"I'm up to a lot of things." He grinned wickedly, rubbing against her hip.

"I'm talking about breakfast."

He kissed her on the lips and sat up on the edge of the bed. "If we must, we must."

"Do you mind?" she asked anxiously.

He lifted his robe from the foot of the bed, wrapped it around him, and belted it. "I know you came home to spend time with your family. It's okay." He walked over to the window and looked out. "Hey, it snowed. There's at least four inches out there!"

She hopped out of bed and stood beside him looking out over the backyard. "The first snow is always so beautiful."

"Do you want to build a snowman?" he asked boyishly.

"And make snow angels?"

"I don't know what kind of angel I'll make, but you've got a deal."

She plucked her pink chenille robe from the bedroom chair and buttoned it. "Do you mind if I spend some time with Dani this morning first? I didn't get a chance yesterday. We can have the afternoon together."

"Lexa, I really don't mind. I'll read the paper, have a few cups of coffee, maybe take a walk. I don't need you to entertain me." His eyes twinkled devilishly. "At least not *all* the time."

She slid her arms under his and hugged him. "Thank you."

"For what?"

"For coming this weekend. For taking time to get to know my family."

"Even if I see some things you don't want me to see?"

"Even then."

"Lexa, you know, don't you, that you can—"

"What?"

"Never mind." The serious look didn't leave Josh's face, but he kissed the tip of her nose. "Let's get moving before I decide I'd rather stay here than play in the snow."

Lexa's father ate breakfast with them, then left for work. Lexa spent much of the morning with Dani, talking and planning. After lunch Dani went to visit a friend who was home for the holidays. Anna was out doing the weekly shopping, and Lexa looked forward to spending the afternoon alone with Josh. She found a pair of old boots in the closet and equipped Josh with her father's galoshes. They walked the grounds, arm in arm, taking in the breathtaking beauty of unspoiled snow.

Lexa insisted they lie down and flap their arms and legs to make snow angels. When they were flat on their backs with snow creeping in their collars, Josh called to her, "Are you sure this is fun?"

"Sure, and it's artistic too. Wait till you see your imprint. Remember to be careful when you get up."

Josh was as careful as he could be, but when he looked at Lexa's angel and back at his, he said with disappointment, "Why doesn't mine look like yours?"

"Because you're bigger and you flapped too hard."

He caught her around the waist and lifted her legs until she was dangling in his arms. She held on tightly around his neck. "You didn't tell me to flap lightly," he complained.

"You didn't ask," she parried with a sassy smile.

He dropped her back on her feet, took a hard kiss, and concluded, "Now we're going to do something *I'm* good at."

Her eyes widened dramatically, and with all the innocence she could muster, she asked, "Out here? Josh, what would the neighbors think?"

He tweaked her nose and swatted her behind. "C'mon, smart aleck. We're going to make one terrific snowman."

They had problems rolling large balls for the body because the snow wouldn't cling. Each ball made a long track on the ground where the grass peeked through. When they finally managed getting three balls into an upright position, Lexa laughed. "It's crooked."

Josh began mounding loose snow onto the second ball. "Never fear, Flannigan's here."

"Oh, right," Lexa muttered drily.

"Don't complain. Go find a carrot for his nose."

Lexa returned not only with a carrot but with an old derby of her father's and a scarf of her own. Josh found stones for eyes. Lexa stood a few feet away from him to admire their handiwork.

"Not bad," Lexa decided. "Now we need a snow woman."

"What for?" Josh teased, his blue eyes sparkling with amusement.

She wagged her finger at him. "What are you, Flannigan? Sexist?"

He pointed to his chest with feigned amazement and questioned, "Me? A man who believes men and women are equal? A man who believes a woman has the right to be president as much as a man, a man who believes—"

Lexa stooped down, patted together a snowball, and cut in, "A man who believes a woman can win a snowball fight?" With careful aim, she threw straight at his chest and the packed snow landed with a splat.

"You're asking for trouble," he warned. When another snowball landed against his shoulder, he shot into action. Within a few seconds, he had packed three snowballs and torpedoed them at her legs. She turned to fashion more of her own. Without taking careful aim, she spun on one foot and threw. Two plastered Josh's stomach, the third exploded on his chin.

"That's it!" he shouted. He took off after her. "Now you're going to get yours."

She ran from him and shrieked over her shoulder, "I was just trying to win."

He was a length behind her. "Now, *I'm* going to win."

She eluded his grasp and raced for the back door. "Did anyone ever tell you you were too competitive?"

He caught the storm door before it slammed in his face, and despite the awkwardness of his galoshes, he almost caught her jacket. When he missed again, he kicked off the boots, shoes and all, and rushed after her up the stairs.

Lexa kicked off her shoe boots in the hall and headed for her room. She had almost managed to close the door when Josh forced it open. She backed up away from him, out of breath and giggling. "It was only a game!"

He closed the door and turned the lock. "We haven't finished this game yet."

Chapter Eight

Lexa scurried away from Josh and stood behind a velvet-covered chair. "I think we could stop now."

He unzipped his jacket and flung it on one post of the four-poster bed. Then he peeled off his socks and unzipped his jeans.

"What are you doing?" she yelped.

"Getting ready to win the game." He smiled smugly.

"Not without a fight." She took off her jacket and tossed it at his head.

He shifted away and pulled his sweatshirt over his head, playfully tossing it to a corner. Lexa cast a glance at the door. He suspected she was calculating how much time it would take to unlock the door and run into the hall. He approached her slowly, not sure which way she'd try to escape.

When she made a run for it, he blocked her, managed to tunnel under the hem of her sweater, and in one swift movement pulled it over her head. As she squirmed and wriggled, he caught her around the waist and pulled her down with him to the bed.

Pinning her hands above her head, he threw his leg over both of hers. "Give up?"

She wiggled, actively trying to break his hold. "Never."

"How did I know you'd say that?" He unfastened her bra and unsnapped and unzipped her jeans.

"What do you think you're doing?" she demanded.

"Putting you in the same condition I'm in," he said lazily. When she tried to raise her shoulders up off the bed, he began a kiss that was exacting, fervent, taming. When he felt her body relax and the tip of her tongue dare to touch his, his hand caressed her stomach. He raised his head and asked huskily, "You don't still want to win, do you?"

She remembered how she had come to be lying on the bed. "You don't play fair," she accused, squirming once more.

He attempted to pull her jeans off with one hand. "Aw, c'mon. Give in."

She tried to roll away from him. "Never."

He pinned her under him and clasped her hands on either side of her head. This time the kiss was pure seduction. He wheedled his way into her mouth and stroked repetitively until her fingers curled between his and the tension went out of her legs. He finished the kiss with a final sweep of her mouth and peppered soft, moist kisses down her neck. Disentangling one hand, he worked her breast, rolling the nipple between his thumb and forefinger until she moaned. When her free hand kneaded his shoulder, he released the other one. While he trailed kisses to her breast, he pushed her jeans down. She rose up to help him and her panties came off too.

Josh kissed her hungrily, exploring every sweet centimeter of her mouth as if he could never get enough. He pressed into her body so she was completely aware of how much he needed her.

Lexa's hands played in the hollow of Josh's back, stroked over his buttocks, trailed as far as she could down the back of his thighs. She aroused him so easily. But she aroused more than physical desire. He wanted to teach her to trust him.

When she undulated against him, he murmured, "Not yet, sweetheart. Not yet."

His hands petted her thighs open, and before she realized his intent, his head lowered to her.

"No," she gasped.

"Yes. Let me know you. Let me know all of you."

When she didn't protest again, he kissed generously, sucked gently. Loving, prodding, provoking.

"Josh, I love you," Lexa breathed.

He thought he'd feel satisfaction when she said it, he thought he'd feel peace. But without her trust, love wasn't enough. He stripped off his briefs, lay on his side, and nudged her to face him. She reached for him, fondling and stroking until he ambushed her mouth again, giving as much as he took.

While their lips clung, he slid her leg over his hip and entered her. Her softness enveloped all of him, thrilling him, exciting him, making him long to take her to heaven and beyond, making him long to destroy all her walls so she could truly be his. He released her lips, moved in and out slowly, and used his fingers on the sensitive spot that pushed her pleasure to its limit.

Lexa murmured, "Oh, Josh. It's so wonderful. Don't stop."

He didn't. As his pulse pounded in his temples, he gave her what she sought. In giving he found his own release.

When he slowly opened his eyes, he saw the wonder on Lexa's face. It was a start. He brushed her hair from her brow and murmured, "I think we both won."

Lexa sorted applications, trying to keep her mind on her work, not on an evening with Josh. She smiled. Since they had returned from her dad's, she had spent two nights at Josh's and he had spent two nights at her place. She loved being with him. They had exchanged keys, and when she returned home from a meeting or volunteer work, he was waiting. It was almost like being married. Almost.

When her phone buzzed, she picked it up. "It's Clare Flannigan," Joanne said. "Line two."

Lexa punched two. "Hi, Clare. How are you?"

"I'm fine. But you might be in for trouble."

"Uh-oh. What did I do now?" she joked.

"Lexa, I don't think this is anything to laugh about. I went to the senior center last night to play cards and I heard from several people that Stanley is furious with you. Somehow he found out what you advised everyone last week and he threatened to sue you for libel and slander."

"He can't do that, Clare. I have as much of a right to advise you to be careful as he does telling you how to invest your money. If he's feeling that threatened, it's even more possible he has something to hide."

"You haven't heard from Josh's friend yet?"

"No, Josh called him yesterday. We could hear anytime. I hope it's sooner rather than later."

"I just wanted to tell you what was going on so you can be on your guard. I don't know if Stanley will confront you or not."

"Thanks a lot. I appreciate it."

Clare's phone call troubled Lexa all afternoon. She wasn't sure whether to confront Stanley herself or remain silent. Her instincts told her to stay away from him. She usually followed her instincts.

With Josh working late because of longer Christmas hours, she stayed at her office after Joanne left, finishing odds and ends. When she finally rose from her desk, her phone rang, but no one was at the other end.

After she put on her coat, she turned out the lights, switched on the security system, and locked the door. She walked to the parking lot, shivering with the blast of icy wind. This was not a fit night to be out. As she approached her car, she saw something on her windshield. At first she thought Josh might have left her a note, but something about her car looked strange. Moving closer, she saw what it was. Fear zipped up her spine as she realized she had four flat tires. With trembling fingers she reached for the paper on her windshield under the wiper. Unfolding it, she read in large printed letters—MIND YOUR OWN BUSINESS. She stared at it a few seconds in shock, letting the wind buffet her. It didn't take Sherlock Holmes to deduce the origin of the note, not after Clare's call.

Lexa looked around the parking lot, across the street,

back to her office, trying to slough off the creepy feeling someone was watching her. She stooped down to look at her front tire. It had been slashed. Thoroughly frightened, she stood and looked around again, seeing nothing but darkness, city lights, and shadows. She heard a rustling in an alleyway, but when she turned toward it, the noise stopped.

Lexa headed for her office at a fast pace, anxious to be in a safe place. Her fingers fumbled with the key as she strove to remain calm, but when she turned on a light, she was shaking all over. *Get a grip on yourself. You have to decide what you're going to do.*

She took three deep breaths. Should she call Mark Gibson at the police station? What if he wasn't there? She could call Josh, but . . .

The phone rang sharply. She studied it, fear gripping her stomach. *You're overreacting, Lexa. Just pick it up.* When she did, again there was no answer. Someone was watching her . . . or at least the lights in her office.

Slumping into her desk chair, she braced her elbows on the blotter and held her head in her hands, trying to think clearly despite the pounding at her temples. She's the one who said she wasn't afraid of Stanley. Had that been sheer bravado or stupidity? Thousands of dollars were involved. What might he do to protect himself? What could she do? She was safe in the office, wasn't she?

The phone rang again and she stared at it as if it were a monster. Slowly lifting the receiver to her ear, she held her breath, expecting to hear a dial tone or a threatening message.

"Lexa, are you there?"

"Josh, thank God . . ." Her voice cracked.

"What's wrong?"

"I . . ." She swallowed her fear and told him what had happened.

"Is the door locked?" he asked with a thread of anger invading his even tone.

"Yes, I made sure when I closed it."

"Don't open it again until you hear my voice. Understand?"

"I have to call the auto club."

"Call them. But do not open the door. I mean it, Lexa. I'll be there in five minutes."

After Lexa called the auto club, she sat in her office, waiting to hear a knock on the door, yet afraid at the same time it wouldn't be Josh.

Five minutes seemed to stretch into five hours. Finally there was a heavy double thump on the door and Josh calling, "Lexa, it's me."

When she stood up, her world spun for a moment then righted itself. She opened the door, and as soon as Josh stepped inside, he engulfed her in his arms. "Lexa, are you all right?"

She rested her head on his shoulder. "I'm fine. I over-reacted."

"You didn't. If I get my hands on Stanley—"

"We don't know if it's him."

"Who else do you think it might be? Do you have a closet full of enemies you haven't told me about?"

"Of course not," she mumbled against his sweater. "I just want to go home."

Josh knew exactly what he wanted to do but decided on what was best to do. He leaned away from her, holding her upper arms. "This has really shaken you up, hasn't it?"

"No, I'm okay. Just tired." Actually, she couldn't think straight.

He was still reacting to her fear. "I'll take you home and we can cuddle up in bed."

Her confusion wasn't helped by the headache pounding in her ears. "I don't need a babysitter," she snapped, more annoyed with herself than the situation.

Josh caressed her cheek. "Believe me, I don't intend to babysit."

She recognized the gleam in his eyes. It brought a wobbly smile to her lips. "I'm really all right. Merely embarrassed you saw me like this."

"Anyone would have been spooked." Flashing yellow lights passed by the window. "That's the tow truck. Let's give him the information he needs so we can go home."

* * *

Josh worried about Lexa as he telephoned the police station. She was upstairs, taking a shower, pretending she was fine. He knew she was scared.

When he got the switchboard, he asked for Mark's extension, hoping he was still in the station.

Mark answered, and without a preamble, Josh explained what had happened to Lexa.

"There's nothing I can do," Mark said when Josh had finished.

"What do you mean there's nothing you can do?" he asked, irritated Mark wasn't more helpful.

"You don't have any proof Stanley was behind it."

"I *know* he's behind it."

"Not good enough. I need hard evidence, not guesses. If you still have the note, I can check for fingerprints, but I doubt I'll find any."

Josh's fist came down on the sofa with his mounting frustration. "Lexa has to be protected. If you won't do something, I will."

"Put it out of your head." When Mark was met by silence, he said, "I mean it, Josh. Don't play the hero."

"What am I supposed to do? Sit back and let her be scared to death?"

"Do you want my honest opinion?"

"You know I do."

"Sure, Stanley's probably behind it. But he feels Lexa is a woman he can scare off with a few threats. Con artists are scared to death of getting caught. That's why they defraud and move on. If Lexa keeps her distance, she'll be okay. I mean it, Josh. I don't feel she's in any danger. Bring the note in and I'll check it. If anything else happens, and you can prove Stanley's involved, of course I'll take action."

"So you're not going to do anything," Josh grumbled.

"There's one thing I can do. I'll notify patrol cars in Lexa's area to keep watch. Will that make you feel better?"

"Some." But not enough. "Thanks, Mark. I know you'll do what you can. Call me as soon as you find out about

Stanley. Anytime." He gave Mark Lexa's number and address. "If I'm not home, I'll be at Lexa's."

Mark tried to be comforting. "Who knows? We might get lucky with those prints."

The next morning, Josh wasn't willing to hope they'd get lucky. He didn't want Lexa in any danger, physically or emotionally. She had awakened in the middle of the night with a nightmare and slept fitfully after that. He hadn't slept much either because he was too busy planning what he was going to do.

After he dropped the note at the police station, he went to Stanley's office. Striding in purposefully, he stopped at the secretary's desk. "I want to see Mr. Stanley. Now," Josh said firmly and calmly.

"I'm afraid that's not possible at the moment. Mr. Stanley's on the phone."

Josh's chin jutted out with determination. "I'll wait. But not long."

"And you're name, sir?"

"Flannigan. Joshua Flannigan."

"This in with regards to . . . ?"

"A personal matter."

When the secretary saw Stanley's phone light go off, she buzzed him. "There's a man here to see you. A Mr. Flannigan."

With a "Send him in," Josh went into Stanley's inner office and ignored his gesture to sit down. "I don't need to sit, Stanley. I came to make one thing perfectly clear. Stay away from Alexandra Kittredge. Don't make any more phone calls, don't go near her office or home, and keep your hands off her property. If you don't, you will have to deal with me and the police department."

"I have no idea what you're talking about, Mr. Flannigan."

Josh knew better. He saw the creases in Stanley's brow, the shift of his eyes, the worry around his mouth. "I know you do. I stopped in to let you know if one intelligent woman can guess your game, it won't be long until others do, too. So watch your step, Stanley."

Stanley recovered his smooth exterior. "Your accusations have no substance, Flannigan. Of course I'm not happy with Ms. Kittredge's ideas of my business acumen. Her comments have been somewhat detrimental. But this is America and everyone is entitled to their own thoughts and expression of them. Now, if you don't mind, I have business to attend to."

Josh lifted the heavy bronze paperweight on Stanley's desk, held it in his palm, looked at Stanley, and set the object back down with a loud thump. "I'll leave. But remember. You step on Alexandra Kittredge's toes, you step on mine." With a last piercing look at Stanley, Josh turned his back and left.

Josh insisted on taking Lexa out to a posh restaurant for a late dinner that evening. She seemed to be her usual self, simply a little quieter. Afterward, he took her to his apartment. When she laid her coat over the back of the sofa, he came up behind her, turned her around, and gave her a bear hug. She burrowed into his shoulder and held tight.

"You can tell me what you're feeling, Lexa."

She leaned back and looked up. "I just feel restless."

He didn't believe that for a minute. "Not afraid?"

"No." She pulled away, frustrated by her need to be held in his arms. She was afraid if she needed him too much, she'd be swallowed up and she wouldn't know her place in the world. As an independent woman, she did. As a person in control of her own life, she did. As a caregiver, she did. This relationship with Josh was stirring up a hornet's nest of needs she had either denied or forgotten.

"It's okay to be scared," he said softly, moving his hands down to cup her elbows.

"I wish you'd stop analyzing what I'm feeling. If I want you to know, I'll tell you."

"Will you? Lexa, don't you understand the relationship I want with you? The kind of sharing? I don't want simply your time. I want you. Why are you fighting me?"

She pulled away from his hands until she was standing

free. "Sometimes I don't know who I am when I'm with you. You make me need and want, and that scares me."

"Tell me when you're scared. I'll do what I can to fix it."

She started shaking her head before he finished speaking. "I don't want you to fix anything. I have to sort all this out, Josh, and I have to do it alone."

He was going to protest, but the doorbell interrupted him.

Lexa asked, "Are you expecting someone?"

"No." Josh answered the door, and let Mark Gibson inside.

The detective said, "I have news for you."

Mark nodded to Lexa. "Hello, Ms. Kittredge. I'm the one who's been looking into Ted Stanley's background."

She motioned for him to sit down while she and Josh sat on the sofa.

Mark took the chair across from them. "I got the lowdown late last night. It seems Mr. Stanley has as many aliases as a tree has branches. He's wanted for fraud in three states and only God knows how many people he's rooked."

"How long has he been doing this?" Josh asked.

Mark looked at the note pad in his hand. "The last five years as far as we can tell. He's never in any hurry. He planned to settle down for a year or so, take in as much as he could, then move on. That's his MO. But something scared him off." Mark gave Josh a speaking glance. "Or someone. When we arrived at his office with a warrant, he was packing up ready to skip town. Any idea why, Josh?"

"How would Josh know?" Lexa asked, confused.

"Got me. What about it, Josh? You were pretty hot under the collar last night."

"Josh?" Lexa asked.

"Look. I knew you wouldn't accept an around-the-clock bodyguard, so I paid Stanley a visit this morning."

"You didn't!" One stark thought crossed her mind. Josh

had put himself in danger for her. "You told me to stay away from him. Why didn't you? Who knows what he might have done."

"Simmer down." Josh capped her knee. "Last night Mark as much as told me con men are cowards."

"I never told you to confront him, Josh," his friend said with a baleful glare.

"I wasn't being foolish. I used the information you gave me and made a calculated decision. All I did was warn him Lexa was off limits."

"You threatened him," Mark translated.

"No. I encouraged him to stay away from Lexa."

"He could have skipped town. I'd have to arrest you for obstructing justice."

When Lexa looked at Josh with astonishment, he squeezed her knee. "This guy's trying to throw his weight around. It makes him feel important."

"The point is—" Mark began.

"The point is," Josh interrupted, "he didn't skip town and you caught him. I am sorry I interfered, but Lexa had to be my main concern."

Mark shook his head and muttered, "Stubborn Irishman."

Lexa couldn't scold Josh when he had her interests at heart. She admired him more than she had ever admired any man. But she was concerned about her friends. "What about the money Stanley took? Will it be returned?"

"When we confiscated his records, we found a slew of checks that hadn't been cashed. My guess is he was going to do it soon, but hadn't gotten around to it. Those checks are null and void. For the ones he did cash, the money can probably be recovered, but claims will have to be made, papers filed, a court process gone through. It will take time."

He stood, his business finished. "I won't take up any more of your time. Both of you have been a big help." He looked at Josh. "Stay out of trouble."

Josh saw Mark to the door. When he returned to the living room, he looked boyishly delinquent.

Lexa couldn't be angry with him. "Thank you."

He sat down close to her. "For what?"

"For protecting me. For putting yourself in danger."

His smile was tender. Instead of replying, he brushed her bangs away from her forehead, and kissed her gently.

Chapter Nine

Lexa snuggled next to Josh the following evening and dipped into a bowl of popcorn while they watched a movie. She'd never felt more contented in her life. She hadn't told Josh again that she loved him since she'd said it in the heat of passion. But she did love him—with all her heart. And that made her even more afraid to tell him her secret.

Every time she started to say it, her tongue stuck to the roof of her mouth. If she told him right now . . .

The telephone rang and she breathed a sigh of relief. Josh pushed the button on the remote, stopping the videotape.

Reaching around him to the end table, Lexa picked up the receiver. "Hello."

"Lexa, it's Dani."

"What is it?"

"I fell. Nothing to worry about. Don't get upset."

"Are you okay? Have you seen your doctor?"

"Yes. This happened last night. He says I'm fine, that babies are well protected. But I'm scared."

"Do you want me to come get you and take you home?"

"I don't want to go home. I want to stay here. Can you come up for a few days? Please?"

"But what about your roommate?"

"She can bunk in with a friend. She says it's okay. Please, Lexa. Can you come up? I do feel okay, but the whole thing scared me. I'd feel so much better if you were here."

Lexa thought about her schedule for the next few days— appointments, meetings, Josh. But the habit of caring for Dani for years won out. "Are you okay for tonight or do you want me to come right away?"

"Tomorrow morning's okay."

"Then I'll leave early tomorrow morning. Take care of yourself, you hear? And call the doctor if you have any problems."

"I will. I'll see you tomorrow."

Josh asked, "What's wrong?"

Lexa told him, then picked up the phone again. "I've got to call my secretary, and do some rescheduling."

Lexa gave her secretary directions and Dani's number, and hung up. Her brow was creased with worry.

"Is there anything I can do to help?" Josh asked.

"No. I have to pack, stop at the office tomorrow morning for some files before I go."

"What time are you leaving?"

"About six."

"Do you have to go so early?"

Lexa hooked her hair behind her ear and picked up a pen and note pad to jot down reminders. "She wanted me to come up tonight."

"Lexa, don't you think you might be overreacting? The doctor said she's okay. I can take you up if you want to spend the day."

Lexa's head jerked up. "Josh, I'm going to stay more than a day. I want to make sure she's taking proper care of herself. A few days of rest will do her good. She'll get that if I'm there. She needs me."

"Does she? Or does she *want* you there?"

"At the moment it doesn't matter." When he frowned,

Lexa said, "Josh, you've never had brothers or sisters. You don't understand how she depends on me."

That was the problem. "She's twenty-one years old. The dependence has to stop sometime."

"It can't stop now. She doesn't have anyone but me."

"I don't believe that, Lexa. Certainly she has friends at college. There are counselors."

"That's not the same. She's my sister. I have to do everything I can."

"As usual."

Lexa gave him a wary look. "What's wrong, Josh?"

He knew he was going to tread on sacred territory.

Lexa went still. "Just say it."

"Dani calls and you go running. I don't think it's good for her and I don't think it's good for you."

Lexa was shaking her head even before he finished. "I don't agree."

"I didn't think you would." He shook his head. "Tell me something, Lexa. If I had called, would you have dropped everything to help me?"

"Of course I would."

His eyes narrowed.

"Don't you *know* that?"

"I know that you do as much as you possibly can for everyone." He debated with himself, then added, "But I'm not sure how your priorities line up."

She put the pen and pad on the coffee table and slid toward him. While she caressed his cheek, she fitted her soft curves into his hard body. "I love you, Josh. Believe me, I do."

He stroked up and down her back. He wanted her to need him. He wanted to come first in her life. Their relationship had to come first for a marriage to be strong. How could he even think about marrying Lexa when she didn't trust him enough to tell him she couldn't have children?

She had to tell him freely. On her own. He just wished she'd do it.

* * *

Josh's lower body stuck out from the cabinet under Clare's sink. His voice was muffled as he stuck his hand out. "Wrench." Clare put the tool in his hand.

A few minutes later, Josh swore. When he emerged from the cabinet, he said, "I'm sorry to tell you this, but I can't fix it. I'm not a plumber."

Clare wagged her finger at him. "Don't you dare say, 'I told you so.'"

He bit back a grin. "I'd *never* do that." At Clare's harrumph, he laughed. "But you'd better call a plumber before that stream under there becomes a river."

"It started with a little drip."

"Most leaks do." He picked up the dishpan on the floor next to him, set it under the dripping pipe, and mopped up small puddles.

After he stood, he washed his hands in the sink. "I can turn the water off for tonight and you can try to get a plumber first thing in the morning."

"All right. I made a chocolate cake today. Would you like a piece?"

Josh glanced at her over his shoulder. "Do I ever turn down your chocolate cake?"

Clare lifted the top on the cake holder. "It was a rhetorical question." She sliced a large wedge. "When's Lexa coming back?"

Turning off the spigot, Josh dried his hands on a towel hanging from the oven door's handle. "She called last night and said she's taking Dani to the doctor's tomorrow to make sure everything's all right before she comes home."

"How did she sound?"

"Tired. I get the impression Lexa's worrying for two, but she won't say so. She's so damned independent."

"Joshua, you wouldn't want a clinging vine." Clare set the large piece of cake on the table.

"No, I wouldn't. But sometimes I'm not sure how much she loves me," he confessed.

"You can measure it?" Clare asked wisely.

"Of course not." He poured himself a full glass of milk. "But if she depended on me a little more . . ."

Sitting down at the table, Clare advised, "Give her some time. She's a loving, intelligent woman. She'll work it out."

Josh pulled out a chair with his foot and sat down. "She's too loving, Clare. She doesn't save much for herself or for us."

"Maybe you expect too much."

"I don't think so." He cut a piece of cake off with his fork and lifted it to his mouth. He swallowed, took a swig of milk, and smiled in appreciation. "Great cake." Scrutinizing Clare carefully, he asked, "So. Despite the plumbing, do you like life here?"

"I love it. I do the cooking. Trudy cleans and we all do the laundry. Jim takes care of the outside work, dishes, and repairs. But plumbing's not his thing either."

"He must be a brave soul living with two women. I bet he doesn't get to say much." Josh noticed a new flicker in Clare's eyes. "Does he?"

Clare ducked her head and wiped a few crumbs from the table. "He says what he thinks."

"And what does he think?"

She met Josh's gaze squarely. "He wants to take me out for lunch this week."

"So go."

She waved her hand in the air as if he were suggesting pure foolishness. "I'm too old for that nonsense."

"*This* is the woman who yelled at me because I thought she was too old for a new venture? Don't you use that as an excuse now."

Her eyes got a faraway look. "So you think I should go?"

"You bet. You only pass this way but once. Go for it."

Clare grinned at her nephew and her blue eyes sparkled. "Maybe I will."

Lexa felt as if she had the weight of the world on her shoulders as she drove home from the college campus. She was worried. Something was going on in Dani's head that she didn't want to talk about. Lexa had prodded, poked, and babied.

They had talked late into the nights—memories of their childhood, their father, their mother, and their step-mother Loretta. Lexa was worn out.

And anxious to see Josh. She had missed him more than she had ever thought possible. But she was tired, so tired. She didn't want Josh to see her when she was feeling so low, but she needed to hear his voice.

She called The Toy Tank as soon as she entered her town house and hung up her coat. When she heard Josh's voice, she felt tears burn in her eyes. She answered his hello with, "I missed you."

His voice was husky. "I missed you too. How's Dani?"

"Okay for now."

"And how are you?"

"Exhausted."

"Do you want me to come over?"

She wouldn't let him see her when she was this down. "No. I have laundry to do, groceries to buy, errands to run."

He heard the strain in her voice. "Are you all right?"

"I'm fine."

"I'll pick you up around six-thirty and we'll go someplace quiet for dinner."

"Josh, if I stop for dinner, I might never get started again. I don't know what kind of company I'll be later."

"Are you saying I shouldn't come over at all?"

"No, of course not. I really missed you and I just want to lie in your arms." Her voice caught, and she strove to steady it and cover up emotions that were too close to the surface. "I'll call you when I get home tonight."

His voice was gentle. "Call me. I'll see you tonight."

After Lexa hung up and lugged her suitcase onto the sofa to take out the used clothes, she sat down next to it and put her fingers to her temples. *What* was wrong with her? Where was her energy? She never had headaches. She went to the kitchen, found a bottle of aspirin in a cupboard, and took two. She was separating the clothes in her suitcase when the doorbell rang. A moment later the door opened and Josh was standing in her living room.

She was so happy to see him, tears gathered in her eyes.

He saw them and in two long strides covered the distance of the room and enclosed her in his arms. Her tears began flowing in earnest, dampening his gray dress shirt.

"Sweetheart, what's wrong?" he asked with concern.

She bit her lip until she gained control. "I don't know. This is so stupid, so foolish." She couldn't stop the tears and she felt ashamed for feeling so weak. Her chin quivered and words stayed stuck on her tongue.

Josh led her to the sofa, held her close to him, and let her cry. "It's okay," he soothed. "Just let it out."

As her tears subsided, she held on to him. He was safety, love, warmth. He probably thought she was a hysterical female. She sat up, turned away from him, dug in her pocket for a tissue, and blew her nose. When she was finished, she knew her nose was red and her eyes were puffy.

"Lexa, look at me," Josh commanded.

When she didn't, he brushed his fingers through her hair, then lifted her chin until her eyes met his.

"Remember our conversation on Thanksgiving after you talked to your father?"

She moved restively. "I remember."

He put an arm around her shoulder. "Let me give to you, Lexa. Learn how to lean on someone other than yourself. That's what loving's all about."

The love in his eyes surrounded her and she felt tears beginning to spill again. "Oh, Josh, I feel so drained. There's no reason for this."

He kissed her forehead and she relaxed against him. "Of course there's a reason for this. I don't think you realize how thin you spread yourself. You have a lot of people making demands on you. Look at what you went through with Stanley. And taking care of someone like Dani is damned hard."

"I love Dani, Josh. I love her baby. I can't help worrying about them. I want this child so badly." Her voice careened around a curve and she let herself recover in Josh's presence, his strength. "I'm glad you're here," she whispered.

His embrace was as strong as his voice was soft. "All you have to do is call me."

She frowned thoughtfully. "That's so hard for me. Even when I was involved with someone before . . . he went his way, I went mine. We were together but separate."

"I don't want that kind of relationship."

"I know, but what you want scares me. It's like losing part of myself."

His large hand caressed her cheek. "Sweetheart, I don't want to take anything from you. I want to give *to* you. Just because you depend on me doesn't make you weak." He traced his forefinger under her eye. It was dark with a blue shadow. "You're exhausted. How much sleep have you gotten this past week?"

"College dorms aren't conducive to sleep."

"Not to mention running yourself ragged for Dani."

She shrugged. "It wasn't like that."

Josh knew better. "Wasn't it?"

Lexa was silent.

"You have black circles under your eyes, you're pale, and you probably need twenty-four hours of straight sleep."

"I can't do that."

His voice grew gruff. "You can, but I know you won't. Compromise and go to bed for a few hours."

Bed did sound good. Cool sheets, the weight of the quilt. She looked at the soiled clothes on the floor in front of her.

Josh picked up a bra and slid his fingers over the delicate beige lace. "I'll do your laundry."

"I can't let you do that."

"Are you afraid your clothes will come out in tatters or ten shades of red?"

She smiled. "I trust your capabilities. But you don't have to."

He stood, took her hand, and pulled her up. "No, I don't have to, but I'm going to."

She capitulated. "Do you know how sweet you are?"

He pulled her to him, gave her an uncommonly eloquent kiss, and gave her a gentle push. "Go upstairs. I'll come up before I leave."

Lexa kissed the top of her finger and held it to his lips. No words were necessary.

She mounted the steps slowly, feeling as if she had run a marathon. After finding a flannel nightgown, she slipped between the sheets and turned on the electric blanket. She was propping herself on two pillows when Josh came in, a mug in hand.

He smiled crookedly, not knowing what her reaction would be. "I thought tea would make you feel better."

"Thank you," she said simply, taking the mug and sipping while Josh partially closed the venetian blinds so the room darkened.

Lexa's eyelids were already heavy. She rubbed the back of her neck, trying to release the tension.

Josh took the mug from her hands and placed it on the nightstand. "Scoot around. I'll massage your shoulders."

The idea of his hands on her shoulders sounded heavenly. She flipped her legs to the empty side of the bed. Josh's thumbs began under her hair, up and down her neck, soothing and loosening. When he started on her shoulders, she sighed with pleasure. Her head dropped down as he worked out the knots with professional skill.

"That feels so good," she murmured. "Where did you learn. . . ? Never mind. I don't want to know."

He patted her back gently. "Lie down and close your eyes." When she was flat on her back, he sat down beside her. "I knew a physical therapist in college."

"Knew?"

His eyes twinkled. "In the technical, not the biblical sense. We were friends."

"Who gave each other massages," she summarized.

"She had to practice on someone," he teased. He straightened the covers under Lexa's chin. "Now go to sleep."

"You'll wake me up when you come back?"

He gave her a considering look. "We'll see."

"Josh . . ." she warned.

"I'll wake you up in time for supper." He kissed her on the lips, waved, and went downstairs.

The room was dark when Lexa awoke from her nap. Light from downstairs illuminated the hall. She pushed her pillows back against the headboard to prop up her head. She was getting her bearings when the bedroom door opened and Josh strode in.

She mumbled, "I'm not awake yet."

"We can postpone supper for a while."

"Josh, I have a meeting at the Y."

He switched on the bedside lamp. "So? There's the phone. Call and tell them you're not coming."

"Josh, I can't. This is important. We're trying to set up a hotline for teens. I said I'd be there."

"You're not going to run yourself into the ground. Call them and tell them you aren't coming."

"You can't order me around!" she fired back.

He scowled at her. "Lexa Kittredge, your compassion is getting in the way of your common sense. You need rest."

He studied her for a long moment. "I understand, Lexa. Believe me, I do. You see human beings who need help, and some fire inside you makes you offer everything you can give. But you can't save the world."

"Damn it, Josh. What I do is important!"

His chin jutted out angrily. "Something has to give. You're about to adopt a baby. That's the most important thing you'll ever do!"

Chapter Ten

Lexa responded softly. "I know what taking responsibility for another life means. I guess I've been trying to cram everything in now before that happens."

A slow smile curved Josh's lips. He sat down next to her on the bed. "You've been focused on other people for so long, you don't know how to give to yourself."

She said huskily, "Are you going to teach me?"

"I'd like to try."

"Josh, I can't just quit everything."

He sandwiched one of her hands between his. "I know that, but if you're thinking about your life, our life, that's the first step."

She looked at Josh and felt so much love, she had to fight tears. "Christmas this year is going to be wonderful."

"Why?" Josh asked, rubbing his finger soothingly over the top of her hand.

"Because of you, because of the baby. I love Christmas. I love the stars in children's eyes, secret smiles, hidden presents, carols, and holly."

"Mistletoe," he included with a lusty look.

She laughed. "Of course." Her feet were getting cold

and she put one on top of the other. "Something happens to people at Christmas. They're nicer to each other."

"I love to watch shoppers. When adults pick out toys, they have as much fun as kids." Josh stooped down and felt her cold foot. "Okay, lady. Either get slippers on your feet or get back under the covers."

"Are you going to be my watchdog?" she asked, not sure what that would mean.

"Nope. But I am going to watch over you. Is that okay?"

"It's okay." She grinned. "But do you think you can let me out of your sight long enough for me to go to the bathroom?"

"Cheekier and cheekier," he sighed with mock dismay as he stood up. "I'm going to fix supper. You be in bed when I get back."

"I'll think about it."

He shook his head as he walked out of the room. "As bad as a kid."

When Josh returned, he was carrying a lap tray with two bowls of chicken soup, three ham and cheese sandwiches, two glasses of milk, and two scrumptious-looking eclairs.

"I take it you're hungry?" Lexa teased.

"So are you."

"Are you trying to convince me?"

"Nope." He wiggled his brows seductively. "I know you have hidden appetites you don't always reveal."

She wrinkled her nose at him. "You think you know me so well."

"I'd like to know you better."

Josh smiled, but his eyes were so serious, as if he knew she was keeping something from him. No, that was impossible.

He fixed the pillows on the other side of the bed and stretched out on top of the covers.

After she ate supper, Lexa couldn't believe how tired she still felt. She thought about getting dressed while Josh took the tray down to the kitchen. When he came back into the bedroom, he was carrying a small portable television. She recognized it. He used it in his bedroom. He set the TV on her dresser, plugged it in, and began to unbutton his shirt.

"What are you doing?"

He stripped off his shirt and started on his jeans. "We're going to relax and watch television. If you fall asleep, that's fine. We're just going to lie here—together."

He picked up Lexa's hairbrush and crawled in beside her. "Come here," he said, patting his chest.

When she laid her head down, he began brushing. The motion was so soothing, she fell asleep.

Opening her eyes, Lexa checked the clock at her bedside. Seven A.M. Josh was sleeping peacefully on his side, his shoulders and arms outside the covers. Whenever she looked at him, something wrapped her heart, tickled it, and made her smile. Until she remembered what she had yet to tell him.

Suddenly, she was struck by the urge to stay home, begin planning the nursery, and maybe spend some of the day with Josh. She reached for the phone. When she called her secretary, the woman assured Lexa she'd hold down the fort another day.

After Lexa hung up, she felt a strong arm curl around her waist. She turned to Josh and smiled. "Good morning."

He pulled her into his arm and cuddled her against him. "Who did you call?"

She ran her hand over his beard-stubbled chin. "My secretary. I'm going to stay home today and take a vacation."

His grin was pleased as his eyes moved over her uplifted face. "Wise decision."

She wanted to melt into his hands when he looked at her like that, but instead of melting, she asked, "Do you think you could get away from the store for lunch?"

"What did you have in mind?"

"I'd like to make something here for you."

"I could take you out for lunch."

"No. I'll make you something here. I thought it might be nice to break up your day."

His hand brushed up and down her arm. "It would be very nice to break up my day. The store's going to be a madhouse. We ran coupons in last night's newspaper and mothers will be out full force today to take advantage of them." He looked at her for a long moment, and she thought she saw the lights of desire in his eyes, but he didn't act on them. He kissed her forehead and shoved himself up. "I'd better get moving."

Was he waiting for her to reach out to him? For her to show him how much she wanted him? She reached up and ran her hand over his shoulder, and down his back. She felt him tremble. "Do you have to leave right this minute?" She wanted to love him and show him how grateful she was for his pampering.

A grin spread from one side of his face to the other. "No."

"Thank you for being here yesterday, for holding me last night."

"Anytime."

She stretched out her arms to him and his gaze told her how much he wanted her to need him, to depend on him. She was learning.

When Josh arrived at Lexa's town house for lunch, he found her in the spare bedroom with wallpaper samples, color wheels with paint shades, and catalogs open to pages of baby furniture.

"Planning to redecorate?" He shifted the mail he'd retrieved from Lexa's mailbox to his left hand.

She started at the sound of his voice. "I didn't expect you this soon."

"It's noon."

Lexa checked her watch under her blouse sleeve. He was right. "Lunch is ready. I made egg salad and cherry cobbler."

"Sounds good." He looked around the room. "What are you going to do in here?"

"Turn it into a nursery. I'm not sure how. Maybe pale yellow walls, this wallpaper on one." She pointed to a pattern with ponies and ducks.

Wanting to draw out his opinions, Lexa pointed to a crib

in the brochure. "I like the maple furniture. Something a child can grow into after he doesn't need the crib. The top of the dressing table comes off and it turns into a chest of drawers."

Josh absently paged through the catalog on the bed. "Kids need so much, don't they? Carriages, strollers, walkers, clothes, toys, car seats And college educations."

"That's a long way off." Lexa didn't really want a generic discussion about babies, but a specific one.

He closed the catalog with a thud. "Not too soon to start saving. Never underestimate compounded interest."

Lexa insisted, "Love's more important."

"Absolutely," he agreed, studying her carefully. So carefully, she asked, "What's wrong?"

"I'm worried Dani will change her mind. I know what you're going to give this child. Can you tell me what you would do if the child's three or four and Dani decides she wants him or her back?"

She pushed her own uneasiness aside. "You're borrowing trouble. That won't happen. Dani won't do that. She couldn't."

"I don't want you to set yourself up."

"I'm not. Trust me, Josh. Trust Dani."

Josh remembered the stack of mail in his hand and offered it to Lexa. "Do I have a choice?"

She saw doubts in Josh's eyes and wished he'd express them. But he didn't. And the moment for sharing secrets had passed. She took the mail from his hand. She ripped open a legal-size envelope and her eyes grew wide with astonishment.

Josh pushed the wallpaper samples out of the way and sat down on the bed beside her. "What is it?"

She rattled the paper in her hand. "This is from Women for a Better America. It's a service organization. Someone nominated me for the award they give each year and I won. Can you imagine? I won!"

"I don't know why you're surprised."

She read the letter again. "But it's such an honor. I know some of the women who won other years. I don't put myself in a class with them."

"You're in a class of your own, sweetheart."

The message in his eyes made her heart beat faster. "You're prejudiced."

"You bet I am." His thumb traced the shell of her ear. "How do you get this award? Do they send it to you or present it to you?"

Her eyes wouldn't leave his face. "There's a dinner at the Holiday Inn on December twenty-second. The mayor will present it then."

He played with her earlobe. "Am I invited?"

Her breathing was becoming shallower. "I can invite ten people. They're giving other awards too."

His hand slid down her neck to her collar. "Am I one of the select group?"

"You're the most select." She cleared her throat. "Are you ready for lunch?"

His eyes glittered suggestively. "I'm more ready for something else."

"Choosing wallpaper?"

"Choosing the slowest, sweetest way of making love to you. This morning was a little too fast. I wanted you badly." Josh began unbuttoning Lexa's blouse. "It was next to impossible to hold you last night and not make love to you."

His words sent a thrill through her. She laid the letter by her side, unknotted his tie, and unbuttoned his shirt collar. "You can do more than hold me now."

He opened her blouse and looked approvingly at her sheer white bra, cupping her breasts gently.

She welcomed his appraisal and his easy touch. Cruising her hand down the middle of his chest, over his stomach to his belt buckle, she murmured, "I want you."

He sucked in his breath and unfastened her bra. "You're the sexiest lady I've ever met."

She battled against the leather as her fingers unbuckled his belt. "You're the sexiest man I've ever met." As he caressed her breasts with soft kneading, she struggled with the zipper on his trousers. Finally she gave up and reveled in the pleasure of his touch. "Joshua Flannigan, do you know how much I want you?"

"Tell me," he said in a low voice.

She swayed toward him. "I want to feel you on top of me. I want to feel you inside me. I want you too much to try to explain."

He laid her back on the bed. "You don't have to explain, love. I know."

She sighed when his lips covered hers. Yes, he did know.

On December twenty-first, the cars in the parking lot at The Toy Tank overflowed from the front parking lot to the back. Lexa found an unoccupied space and walked through scattered snow flurries to the front door. She wanted to surprise Josh.

She had been Christmas shopping, battling crowds to find exactly what she wanted. Josh had been a challenge. She had finally decided on an original watercolor of three clowns performing for a child. She had been drawn to the painting and knew Josh would love the spirit of it.

As Lexa entered the store, she pulled off her knit tam and let her hair fly free. Stuffing her gloves in her pocket, she went to find Josh. Children were everywhere, chattering, laughing, crying. Adults were hurrying patiently and impatiently because they only had fifteen more minutes to shop before the store closed.

When Lexa opened the door to the small office, the manager smiled, and told Lexa she could find Josh in the back corner of the store.

At first all Lexa saw was Santa's throne, a box shaped and decorated like a chimney holding oranges for the children who sat on Santa's lap, and a basket of candy canes. She took a closer look at Santa. Her lips curved and she nearly laughed aloud as she recognized the face beneath the white beard.

Lexa watched Josh as he helped a small boy about four years old onto his lap. He held the boy with one strong arm as he asked in a deeper voice than usual, "What's your name?"

The boy put one finger in his mouth and looked at Josh

intently. Then he seemed to decide he could trust him and volunteered, "Timmy."

"Well, Timmy. Tell me what you like to do."

Timmy's brown eyes sparkled. "I like to ride my big wheel, but it's too cold outside so I ride in the basement."

"And what else do you like to do?"

Timmy's index finger went into his mouth again as he thought. "I like to help Daddy build stuff. He's a carpenter," Timmy said proudly.

"Do you have any brothers or sisters?" Josh asked.

"Yeah. A sister. She's in fourth grade. She didn't want to come see you. She says she doesn't hafta ask Santa Claus for what she wants. She thinks I'm a baby."

"But you're not, are you? I bet you help your mom and dad a lot."

"Sometimes I help Mom empty the dishwasher and water the plants. She said to tell you I'm usually pretty good."

Josh looked up and found Timmy's mother smiling at him. He ruffled the boy's hair.

"So what would you like for Christmas, Timmy?"

The boy swung his legs back and forth, making his balance on Josh's knee precarious. "I want a real bicycle. Red. With training wheels. That's what I really want."

Josh saw the affirmative nod from Timmy's mother. "I don't think that's too much to ask for a pretty good boy like you. Was there anything else?"

Timmy screwed up his nose. "I'd like a hamster. A brown furry one in a house with lots of rooms. I saw one on TV."

Josh caught the negative signal from Timmy's mom. "You know, you might be a little young for a hamster. You'd have to clean out his cage every week, never forget to give him food and water. Are you ready to do all that?"

"I don't know if I can. I can't reach the sink. I really want a pet. How about a kitty?"

Through his fake spectacles, Josh watched Timmy's mother shrug and mouth "okay."

"I think you could take care of a kitten. Do you think your mom will help you?"

Timmy turned to his mother and she nodded. "Sure.

She'll help. And when I'm five, I can do everything all by myself."

Josh chuckled. "I bet you will." He picked up an orange and a candy cane, gave them to Timmy, and helped him down. "You have a Merry Christmas."

Timmy waved his candy cane. "I will. Thanks, Santa."

Aware of the store closing in a few minutes, Josh held out his arms to the last child in line, a little girl about two years old. She couldn't make up her mind whether she wanted to laugh or cry. He held her loosely and asked gently, "What's your name?"

She reached out and touched his beard. "Soft!" she exclaimed and giggled.

"It tickles, too," he told her with a smile. "What's your name, honey?"

She looked for her mother to make sure she was close by. "Tina." She wriggled down off of Josh's lap. Her mother picked her up and said, "Tell Santa what you want for Christmas."

"Wanna dolly," Tina said.

Lexa could tell Josh was having a hard time not laughing.

"What else, baby?" the mother prodded.

"Blocks," Tina answered.

"Legos," the mother clarified. "She just loves to build things. I'm sure she's going to be an architect."

Josh held up a candy cane and an orange to Tina. She grabbed the candy. Her mother took the orange. Tina's hand fluttered at Josh as her mother carried her away. Josh's demeanor and his ease with the children filled Lexa with joy. All at once, she knew that Josh would love Dani's child as much as he would love a child of his own. He had so much love to give and he knew how to give it. He would be a terrific father.

Josh, unaware of Lexa, sat watching the mother and child walk away. The store was quiet except for the cash registers up front. Lexa walked over to Josh, and before he knew what was happening, she settled in his lap with her arms around his neck. "Hi, Santa. Can I tell you what I want for Christmas?"

He fell in with her game. "I don't know. You're an awfully big girl. Do you still believe in Santa Claus?"

"I'll always believe in Santa Claus. And I'm not so big," she protested.

His hand slid under her coat, slid down her hip and thigh. Then he jiggled her on his legs, endangering her balance. "Not too big, not too small. I guess I could say you're just right."

She hung on tighter. "Just right for you."

He laughed. "You should know. Especially after last night."

"Santa! We don't talk about things like that in public."

He checked the area around them. "I don't see any public."

She poked him in the stomach. "Are you going to listen to what I want for Christmas?"

"How long is this list?" he asked suspiciously.

She pondered his question. "About two pages."

"Shorten it. This suit is getting hot. Let alone the rash I'm probably getting from the beard."

"Oh, the disadvantages of being Santa Claus," she sympathized.

"I can tell you really feel sorry for me."

She wiggled on his lap. "More and more every minute."

He tickled her. "Sit still if you want to tell me what you want for Christmas."

She behaved for the moment. "I'll just list the most important. I want at least ten kisses a day, twelve hugs, a massage once a week, and an egg slicer."

"An egg slicer?" he repeated.

"It'll be easier to make you egg salad."

"Of course. I should have thought of that," he joked. "Now about your other wishes. You realize I'm the only Santa Claus that can deliver hugs, kisses, and massages to you."

"That's acceptable."

"Only acceptable?"

She kissed him with his beard tickling her chin and nose. "*Very* acceptable."

"My glasses are steaming up. Let's go upstairs so I can get this suit off."

She hopped off his lap. As soon as they walked through the double doors to the stock room, Josh flicked off his hat and beard. He took Lexa in his arms. "Now I want a real kiss."

"I don't give artificial ones," she returned smartly.

His kiss punished her for her impudence and praised her for her femininity, but when he drew her into his body, he couldn't feel her against him. "Damn. I've got to get out of this suit."

She giggled. "I always wondered how it would feel to make love to Santa Claus."

"Not very satisfying."

"You don't know that. Someday you might have a beer belly."

"Heaven help me."

"I'd still love you," she said, tentative as she suddenly realized that, more than anything else in the world, she wished for a marriage proposal from Josh.

His blue eyes were serious. "Would you?"

They stared at each other, probing the depths of their love. Josh's voice was gravelly when he said, "Let's go upstairs."

When they reached the top of the stairwell, Josh opened the door to his apartment and let Lexa pass through. They stopped in Josh's bedroom. He unbuckled his wide black belt, threw it to the chair, and unbuttoned the red jacket. "What are you doing here, anyway? I thought you had a meeting at the Y."

"I did."

He took the padding out of his jacket. There was a note in her voice that made him look at her speculatively. "It must have been a short meeting." He shucked off the jacket and unzipped the pants.

"I didn't go." She stood perfectly still by his dresser to wait for his reaction.

Josh kicked off the cumbersome black boots and stepped out of the pants. "Why not? Was it canceled?"

She stared at his long, powerful legs, the beauty of his

male body. "No. I called the coordinator and told her I wouldn't be able to attend any more meetings."

Josh laid the red pants on the bedroom chair, propping the boots beneath it. "Did you tell her why?" His inflection said he wanted to know himself.

Lexa waited until he was standing straight, facing her. "I told her my personal life needed more attention."

He approached her slowly. "Exactly what does that mean?"

"I'm going to stay involved at the senior center and give one night a week to tutoring. The rest of the nights are ours."

He grinned. "I thought *I* was Santa Claus."

She spread her fingers on his shoulders, appreciating the hardness, his strength. "What do you mean?"

He began unbuttoning her silk dress. "That was one of my wishes for Christmas, but I didn't think it would happen."

"Josh, I love you."

He caressed her cheek with the back of his hand.

"I love you, too, Number One Elf."

She felt closer to Josh tonight than she'd ever felt. He held out his hand to her and she took it. She'd love him the best way she knew how, and maybe afterward she'd find the courage to tell him about her sterility.

Chapter Eleven

Josh sat in Tom Norman's office, examining blueprints for the expansion of his store. He tapped his forefinger on a white line. "I like the special section for CDs, tapes, and books."

The husky contractor puffed on his cigar. "Yeah. More stores oughta push them instead of videos. The boob tube is making kids lazy. One night a week we turn it off and everyone settles down with a book. Even me and my wife. You married?"

Josh had had several meetings with Tom, and the contractor had inspected Clare's house. But they'd never talked about anything more than business. "No, not yet."

"Don't rush it." Norman poked his cigar at Josh for emphasis. "Lucky for us men, there's no hurry. We can have kids in our seventies."

"I don't think I want to wait that long," Josh said with a smile. "Anyway, kids aren't the only reason to get married."

Tom shrugged his brawny shoulders. "No, maybe not. My wife and me, we still go to the movies, out to dinner. She tells me we have to, so when the kids all move out, we won't be strangers."

"Have you been married long?"

"Eighteen years."

"That's a long time." Josh wondered what Lexa would look like eighteen years from now. With her classic beauty, she'd age gracefully.

"Yep. When we hit twenty-five, we're gonna take one of those cruises around the Caribbean. Ever been there?"

"No, I haven't." But it would be a great place to honeymoon. He and Lexa could go to Saint Thomas, Martinique, or maybe she would prefer Hawaii. In a flash Josh realized he had decided he was going to ask Lexa to marry him . . . now . . . tonight. Maybe then she could tell him. Maybe then she'd realize he'd love her, children or no children.

Tom Norman motioned to the blueprints. "So everything here meets your approval?"

Happiness stirred Josh's heart as he brought his attention back to Tom and kept his excitement in check. "Sure does. You've done a good job."

"I'll get back to you in a couple of days about a start date. Are you going to be around over Christmas?"

After he asked Lexa to marry him, he didn't know what she'd want to do. She might want to go to Philadelphia for a few days. "I'm not sure. If I go out of town, I'll give you a call."

Tom rolled up the blueprints and stuffed them in a cardboard tube. "That's fine."

Josh had a stop to make at the jewelers before he went home to change for Lexa's award dinner. He extended his hand and shook Tom's. "I'll be waiting to hear from you."

Josh left Norman's office with a sense of urgency. This was it. The most important night of his life. He couldn't wait for it to begin.

Lexa heard the apartment door shut and she called to Josh from his bedroom. "I'm in here. We're both running late." When he appeared in the doorway, she asked, "Have you been with the contractor again?"

She was pulling sheer pantyhose up her legs. The sight

was pleasurable, and as always when he looked at her, desire stirred. "Yes. And I had to do some last-minute Christmas shopping."

Lexa stood to adjust the elastic around her waist. "For me?" she asked impishly.

His attitude was smug. "Maybe." The box in his pocket was for Christmas, but he'd ask the question tonight. He stripped off his shirt and trousers. "But it's not for you to be concerned with right now. Are you jittery about the dinner?"

Pulling the strapless slip over her head, Lexa let it slide into place. "I had an acceptance speech all prepared, but the more I think about it, it sounds stilted."

Josh riffled through his closet for a clean white shirt. "Just say what's in your heart. You don't need a speech."

Lexa had decided to dress at Josh's so they could leave together. She was glad she had. She could share her excitement but calm her nerves. She took a flame-colored dress from its hanger and dropped it over her head, but she had trouble trying to raise the back zipper.

Josh pulled up the zipper, ran his hands up her exposed back, and buttoned the button at the back of her neck. Turning her around, he placed his hands on her hips and with undisguised desire viewed the halter top clinging seductively to her breasts.

"Alexandra Kittredge, you're enough to drive a man out of his mind. I don't think I want anyone else ogling you."

Lexa trailed her fingers down the middle of his chest, stopping at the waist of his trousers. "And you're too handsome for your own good. When the women at this shindig see you . . ." She affected a sigh and rolled her eyes.

"Then we're the perfect couple. So perfect that maybe we should do something about it."

"We don't have time," she joked.

"That wasn't what I had in mind." He could see she didn't understand. He wondered why the words were suddenly so hard to get out. What if she said no? What if she didn't *want* to get married? They hadn't talked about it.

"Josh?" she asked.

His hands tightened on her waist. "I want to know if you'll marry me."

The hoarseness of his voice, the importance of the question, made her knees weak. "What?"

"What do I have to do? Get down on one knee? Will you marry me?"

"Are you sure?" she asked breathlessly.

"I'm sure. I've never been more sure of anything in my life. I love you, Alexandra Kittredge. More than I ever thought possible. I want to set up housekeeping, go on a honeymoon, and start preparing to raise our family." His whole body was tense until she threw her arms around his neck and he heard, "Yes, Josh. Yes. I'll marry you. Of course I'll marry you."

His lips swooped down and kissed hers with bruising intensity. His tongue darted into hers, passionately stroked, lovingly swept until they were both breathing raggedly. When he released her, he said huskily, "This is the damnedest time to be going to a dinner."

She smiled shakily and suddenly looked worried. "Maybe it won't last too long."

"Fat chance," he muttered. "I was going to wait until we came home, but I couldn't hold it in."

"I'm glad." She stroked his cheek. "I love you, Josh. I want to be your wife. When we get home, I'll show you exactly how much."

"You think knowing that is going to help me get through an evening with you sitting across the room? Not even close enough to touch?"

"The touching will come later," she promised.

"You're not helping, Lexa," he growled.

She smiled coyly and let her hands roam across his shoulders. "Are you complaining?"

"I am. I want to make love to you *now.*"

She dropped her hands and stepped back. "All good things come to those who wait."

"You're a tease," he grumbled, brought her into his chest for a hard kiss, then intentionally set her away. "Finish dressing before I decide to undress you."

A half hour later, Josh sat at a table with Clare and other

people with whom Lexa had worked on various committees. He made polite conversation but kept his eyes on Lexa as she spoke with the mayor, who was seated on her right, and another award recipient on her left. He marveled at the way she could make herself at home anywhere with anyone. He imagined her with a baby in her arms, her eyes glistening with love as she rocked a child—their child—to sleep. She was a remarkable woman who would make a remarkable mother.

Clare elbowed Josh. "You're staring."

Josh grinned. "That lady's going to be my wife."

"Does she know that?" Clare inquired with a smile.

"I asked her tonight and she said yes. So you can go shopping for something to wear to the wedding."

"Have you set a date?" Clare asked.

"Not yet. But I want it to be soon. There's no reason to wait."

"If Lexa wants a church wedding or a reception, you might *have* to wait."

"Then we'll elope. No fuss, no bother."

"Now, Josh. A wedding day is the most important day in a woman's life. Don't deprive Lexa of the joy and excitement."

"Can't she have the joy and excitement without a big production?"

"Maybe."

Josh took the napkin from his lap and placed it on the table. "We'll do whatever she wants. I want to make her happy."

Clare looked at her nephew fondly. "With that attitude, you will."

The president of Women for a Better America tapped the microphone for quiet, introduced herself, and began. "I'd like to present to you the recipient of our Service Award. This woman has chosen a service career. A career that is more of a vocation than a means of earning a living. I have known Lexa for three years and I can't begin to count the number of people she has counseled and for whom she has found employment. But she doesn't stop there. She carries her skills and expertise into her free time.

"Lexa has done more than anyone else in our community to better the lives of our senior citizens. And without further ado, I present to you this year's Service Award recipient, Alexandra Kittredge."

Lexa walked to the podium with her knees shaking. She'd forgotten her prepared speech.

She reached the lectern. The lights were bright, the microphone daunting. She tried to still her trembling, but her hand shook when she rested it on the wood surface. She looked out into the crowd, and she spotted Josh. His eyes were shining, steady, and they spoke to her. *You're fine. You're mine.* She knew in her deepest heart she wanted to be his forever.

She smiled directly at him and realized her prepared speech didn't matter. What mattered was what she truly felt in her heart and how much Josh meant to her. "I want to thank everyone who helped make this award possible. I haven't done any of this alone. Despite red tape, people came together and made something happen. Whether we are feeding the hungry, helping to improve living conditions, or giving teens a place to go to have wholesome fun, we are people helping each other. I used to feel that compassion was all that was necessary. As long as we had compassion and cared enough, the world could change. But in the last few months I've discovered compassion has a friend." She paused. "That friend is love."

Her voice gaining strength, she continued, "When we are surrounded by love, our compassion has new meaning. It might be more selective, but it has a greater strength. Combined with love, our compassion can give others our best, the very essence of who we are. I want to thank all those people who have supported me, encouraged me, and loved me."

She held up the award and looked straight at Josh. "Thank you for helping me learn how to receive as well as give. Because in receiving, I can give more."

When she left the podium, the audience applauded. Josh felt proud enough to burst. He loved this lady, and he welcomed the happiness he experienced at her achievement. And he hoped when they got home tonight, she could truly open her heart to him.

By the time Lexa extricated herself from admirers and well-wishers, she just wanted to go back to Josh's apartment and be held in his arms. In the car they didn't speak as Josh laid his hand on Lexa's knee and she caressed the top of his fingers. After he parked at his apartment, he opened her door for her, wrapped his arm around her waist, and walked her up the stairs.

After Josh closed the door, he flicked on the light and stared at Lexa. She unbuttoned her coat and laid it over the sofa. Because he was still staring at her intently, she asked, "What?"

"Do you know how proud I was of you tonight?"

"No."

"I wanted to stand up and shout, 'This terrific lady is going to marry me.'"

"Oh, Josh." She gave him a kiss that was ineffably tender.

Josh's body responded to her gift. He spread his legs, pulled her into himself, and caressed her back slowly, stroking in sensuous circles until she rubbed her breasts against him to create more excitement.

His fingers were fumbling with the button at the back of her neck when the telephone rang. When the jangling persisted, he tore away and swore graphically.

"You better get it," Lexa whispered.

Josh dashed his fingers haphazardly through his hair and took a deep breath. "Right," he said gruffly as he picked up the phone. After saying hello and listening for a few seconds, he held out the receiver to Lexa. "It's Dani."

Lexa's brows shot up and Josh shrugged. She took the phone from his hand. Josh listened as she talked.

"Dani, what's wrong?" Lexa's face lost all its color. "You can't! What if he walks out again?" Lexa's thumb rubbed between her brows as if she had a headache. "I'll be home as soon as I can. Dani, please don't make a rash decision. We have to talk. Okay?"

When Lexa hung up the phone, Josh was by her side. "What happened?"

Her voice wasn't quite steady. "Rob has changed his mind. He wants to marry Dani and she's going to keep the baby."

Josh put his arms around Lexa and held her. After a few minutes, she leaned back. "I can't believe that she thinks he means it. He didn't stand beside her before. Why does she think he will now?"

"Maybe he's had a change of heart."

"Oh, puh-leez," she drawled sarcastically as she pulled out of his embrace so she could think clearly.

"Lexa, you usually give people the benefit of the doubt."

"Not when they're playing with other people's lives. What if Rob doesn't realize he doesn't want the responsibility after the baby's born and then walks out?"

An involuntary grunt escaped Josh's mouth. "That's the worst possible scenario."

"Yes, it is. And Dani has to realize it could happen."

"Have you ever met Rob?" Josh asked, wanting to reassure Lexa and comfort her without knowing how.

"I've spoken with him three or four times. Material success is important to him. All he wanted to do was graduate and get a job with an ad agency in New York. Now Dani tells me he's going to go into his dad's business after graduation. His dad sells cars and Rob's going to do the PR work. How long is he going to be satisfied with that?"

Josh's heart ached for Lexa. She was denying what she didn't want to accept. "Maybe he realizes a wife and family are more important than a high-powered job."

Lexa backed away from Josh and eyed him warily. "Why are you defending him?"

"Maybe he needs a chance to prove himself."

She wrapped her arms around herself, as if trying to ward off a chill. "And what about Dani? What if she trusts him and he doesn't deserve her trust?"

Josh's eyes caught hers and held tight. "Lexa, *she* has to make this decision. You can't make it for her."

Suddenly cold, she rubbed her arms. "What they do affects us. I *want* this baby."

Josh spoke quietly. "Lexa, it's Dani's baby."

Her hands dropped to her sides. She paced across the

room to the window and looked out, afraid to face the truth in his eyes. More to herself than to him, she murmured, "But she said she didn't want to keep it. She said she couldn't."

"Now she can."

Lexa wheeled around to face him. "How can you take this so calmly? You don't understand what this means. I can't . . ."

"Can't what, Lexa?"

She couldn't hold back a sob. "I can't have children."

"I know. I overheard you when you were talking to Dani."

"You knew? And you didn't tell me you knew? I've been worrying and worrying—"

"You could have confided in me a long time ago."

"I was afraid you'd walk out."

"Lexa, we can adopt. Dani's decision to keep her baby could be the best decision for all of us. If she'd made this choice after the baby was born, you'd only have more heartache."

"Don't you understand?" Her eyes became dark pools of sorrow. "This is my one chance to have a child, maybe my only chance. Adoptions can take years *if* they approve you. They wouldn't consider me at all if I were single."

"You won't be single, will you?"

Suddenly Lexa wasn't sure of anything. Josh loved children. How could they have a life without them?

"Did you want this baby? Could you have accepted it as your own?"

He raked his hand through his hair. "Yes. I love kids."

"So what happens now, Josh? You love children. I might not be able to have children." She rubbed her hands together anxiously. "Doesn't that affect how you feel about me? About us?"

He slashed his hand through the air. "For God's sake, Lexa. I love *you*. We have each other."

Tears rose in her throat and her heart pounded vehemently. "Will that be enough? Won't you hurt every time you see a couple with a child? How can your love last through that?"

He made a move toward her but she put up her hands to ward him off. Standing still, he stuffed his hands in his pockets. "It can, but only if you trust me. I know you're upset. But there *are* other alternatives you haven't considered. Why have you tied up all your hopes in Dani's baby?"

"I don't understand what you're getting at."

Taking his hands out of his pockets, he sat down on the arm of the sofa. "Maybe you're upset about more than losing this child."

She was too agitated to sit or to see Josh's reasoning. "You're not making sense."

"I am." He rested his hands on his knees, as if his calm could somehow calm her. "You saw adopting Dani's child as another way to take care of her, to protect her."

Her breath whooshed out of her lungs as if he had punched her in the stomach. "Josh, no! I wanted this baby!"

"You can't take responsibility for Dani forever. You don't have to for her to love you. Lexa, can't you realize you don't have to keep doing things or taking care of people to be loved?"

"Yes, I care what happens to other people. I thought you finally understood that, but maybe you don't. And if you don't understand me, we shouldn't be considering marriage."

He stood up stiffly. "You don't mean that."

"Yes, I do. We both need time to think, to be sure we have a future together."

"Lexa, we don't need time. We need to talk this out."

"I can't, Josh. Not now. I have to go to Dani and find out if she's sure about this. I have to find out what she wants."

"What about what *I* want, Lexa? What about our future? Aren't we *as* important? More important? Because if we aren't, we have nothing to build on."

A tear rolled down her cheek followed by another. "Josh, I feel as if I'm being pulled ten different ways and I have to sort it out. But I can't do that until I talk to Dani and Rob. They're at my dad's and that's where I'm going."

He looked at her as if she was out of her mind. "You're not serious about going tonight."

She lifted her coat from the sofa and put it on. "Yes, I am. As soon as I get packed."

His question was clipped. "When will you be back?"

She turned away and picked up her purse. "I don't know."

"Lexa, I can't come with you tonight. This close to Christmas I'd have to make some arrangements . . . at least give it a day or so."

"I'm not asking you to leave, but I am asking you to understand. I have to go to Dani. Tonight. Please, Josh, try to see—"

He cut in harshly. "Go if you have to."

"Josh . . ." He made no move toward her and she couldn't move toward him. She walked to the door and put her hand on the doorknob. He said nothing. She opened the door and walked out into the cold winter night.

It was three in the morning when Lexa arrived at her father's. He was sitting in the living room, staring into the fire, when Lexa let herself in. She left her suitcase and coat in the foyer and went to sit beside him on the sofa. Donald Kittredge took one look at his daughter and opened his arms. There was no way Lexa could stop her tears.

"Honey, for your sake, I wish this hadn't happened."

Lexa swallowed a sob and raised her head. "Dad, isn't there anything I can do, anything I can say to convince her?"

"Lexa, this is between you and Dani. All I can say is don't let it destroy your relationship with her. I talked to her and Rob and they didn't come to this decision lightly. I saw a strength in Dani tonight that has never been there before."

"Dad, I wanted this baby so much."

"I know you did. This seemed like the perfect solution to you, but it was too perfect. I know I wasn't around much, but I saw what often happened between you and Dani.

Dani got into jams; you got her out of them. I'm not saying that was wrong, but maybe it kept her from growing up."

"Do you think I pushed her into this?"

Her father was frank. "No. I think she was confused and you handed her a solution. But it wasn't the right solution."

"I might never have a baby." Her eyes were desolate. "I might never have a child to raise."

"Maybe not a baby, Lexa. But there are children out there that no one wants. There are older children who are hard to place. Have you considered what you could give to one of them?"

Her father had given her something to think about. She leaned back against the sofa, letting her head lie heavily against the cushion. "I could offer a lot. So could Josh."

"It would also give you and Josh more time to be alone together before that happens." Donald seemed to sense Lexa was worried about something else. "What's wrong?"

She sat up. "I was at Josh's when Dani called."

"And?" he prodded.

"I was shocked, numb, upset. I . . . . I came here instead of staying with him. He thinks I don't trust him. He might never forgive me for walking out."

"Never's a long time."

"This was serious, Dad. Earlier tonight he asked me to marry him. Then when Dani called, I told him we might never have any children."

"Just tonight?"

"Yes. But he already knew because he overheard me talking to Dani when we were here." She suddenly realized something tremendously important. "He asked me to marry him and he already knew."

Donald patted Lexa's leg. "That should tell you how much he loves you."

"He *did* love me. I don't know if he still does."

"Trust him, honey. Trust in his love."

Donald Kittredge's words kept ringing in Lexa's ears as she slept for a few hours, wakened, and dressed. Yesterday's events had helped her understand that Josh's love was *the* most important thing in her life. It mattered more than anything else. The thought of losing that love scared her to death. She picked up the phone to call him, but put it back down. What she had to say, she had to say in person.

When Lexa entered the kitchen, Dani was eating a breakfast of toast and tea. Dani glanced at her sister nervously. "Lexa, I know how much this has probably hurt you. But I *had* to make this decision. I don't want to lose you, but I have to keep my baby."

Lexa poured herself a cup of coffee and carried it to the bar. "It's always been you and me against everyone else. We had each other and we didn't let anybody else in."

"You're sorry we're close?" Dani asked, her eyes filling with tears.

Lexa climbed on a stool next to her sister. "No, I'm not sorry about that."

Dani fingered the handle of her butter knife. "I let you take care of me, do things for me, because it was easier to let you solve my problems so I didn't have to. I knew what I was doing, Lexa, even if you didn't."

"We were using each other."

"How did you use me?" Dani asked, turning on the stool to face Lexa.

"Fixing things for you made me feel important. It would have been harder for me to stand back and let you make mistakes."

"Lexa, I don't feel my baby's a mistake anymore. Maybe I never did. I think I wanted to get pregnant to force Rob to make a commitment. When it didn't work, I got scared and didn't know what to do."

Lexa turned her mug in a circle. "So I came to your rescue. Again."

"Yes. But this time something wasn't right. I didn't like the way you solved it. Do you know what I mean?"

"I think so. Your heart was telling you one thing, and I was telling you another."

"That's it. Even if Rob hadn't changed his mind, I couldn't have given up the baby. When I fell and I thought I might lose it . . . After that, well, I didn't know how to tell you. And then when Rob came knocking on my door one night, it was like a dream come true."

"This is reality, Dani."

"I know that. Believe me, I know we both have some growing up to do." Dani's face became animated. "But we want it to work. Rob really loves me, Lexa. I know he does. And he loves our child too."

Lifting her mug to her lips, Lexa took a small sip. "I was furious with you last night. I wanted the baby badly because it might be my only chance. But this is the one time in your life you should stand on your own two feet and tell me to butt out." Lexa set down her mug and her eyes grew shiny. "I've always loved you, Dani, but now I respect you for doing what your heart knows is right."

This time Dani reached out and took Lexa's hand. "I love you, sis."

Lexa realized they were treating each other as equals for the first time. From now on, they would be not only sisters, but friends.

Chapter Twelve

On the afternoon of December twenty-fourth, snow
flurries spilled from the early afternoon sky. Lexa had
driven back to Chambersburg, exceeding all speed limits.
But Josh wasn't at the store. He was at a business meeting.
And suddenly she was nervous. Maybe she needed to do
more than turn up on his doorstep.

Lifting the heavy brass knocker on the solid wood door
of Friendship House, Lexa hoped Clare was home. For
someone who never sought out advice, Lexa was learning
how. Her father had given her important insights. Now
she needed Clare's opinion.

After a few moments, the door opened and Clare
exclaimed, "You're back!"

"Yes, and I need to talk to you. Do you have a few
minutes?"

Clare took her arm and almost pulled her inside. "Josh
has been a bear. He wouldn't tell me when you'd be back."

"He didn't know."

After Lexa removed her coat, Clare led her to the
kitchen. "I'll put on a pot of tea. You must be frozen
through."

Lexa sat at the table while Clare put the water on to

boil. "Are you ready for Christmas?" Lexa didn't feel like making small talk but she couldn't jump right in.

"As ready as I'm going to be. I have two more presents to wrap." She gave Lexa a probing glare. "But you're not here to talk about me. Does Josh know you're back?"

Lexa met Clare's eyes. "No. I called the store. The sales manager told me Josh was gone for the afternoon. He had an appointment with the contractor."

"Are you going to see him tonight?"

Lexa was too restless to sit. She stood and paced the kitchen. "Yes, but I'm not sure how he feels."

"You're not going to find out until you talk to him."

Lexa stopped at the refrigerator and took out a lemon. "I thought he might have spoken to you."

Clare smiled sympathetically. "Are you using me as a barometer?"

"I guess so." Lexa took a cutting board from the hook on the wall and set it on the counter. "In the last few weeks, I've discovered my father's someone I didn't know, my sister needs to stand on her own two feet without my interference, and Josh . . . I love him more than I ever thought I could. Did you know he asked me to marry him?"

"He told me at your dinner. He couldn't help it; he was ready to burst."

"I disappointed him. I might have destroyed what we had."

Clare opened the tea canister and removed two tea bags. "I saw him last night. He stopped for a while. Lexa, I'm sorry about Dani and the baby. I can understand why you thought you had to leave right away."

"I shouldn't have been so impulsive. I should have waited for Josh to go with me. He probably thinks I don't want to marry him."

"Do you?"

"More than I want anything. But I don't know what he's thinking and feeling. Did he tell you . . ."

"That you can't have children? Yes. He said that's why you were so upset you couldn't adopt Dani's baby."

"Do you think he truly doesn't care about having children?'' Lexa cut the lemon into thin slices. "I don't want to marry Josh and deprive him. He's so good with kids."

The teapot whistled and Clare turned off the gas burner. "What did Josh say?"

Lexa took two mugs from the wooden tree and set them on the table. "He says it doesn't matter. He says we have each other."

Pouring water into the cups, Clare said, "Believe him. Lexa, I raised that boy. I know him almost as well as I know myself. He's a tad stubborn, he gets angry a bit too easily when it's something he cares about, but he's an honest man. He doesn't say what he doesn't mean."

In the depths of her soul, Lexa knew Clare was right. Josh might be angry with her, but he wouldn't stop loving her. Her own doubts and fears had prevented her from trusting his love.

Lexa sat at the table, swinging her tea bag back and forth in the mug. "I have to convince Josh I love him, and I want to be his wife. I'll do anything to prove it. Do you have any ideas?"

Sitting down across from her, Clare asked, "Do you have a key to his apartment?"

Lexa felt her cheeks get hot. "Yes."

Clare smiled knowingly. "This is the nineties, Lexa. I don't live in a cocoon."

Lexa cleared her throat. "What do you have in mind?"

"You could have a nice dinner waiting as a peace offering when he comes home."

Lexa figured a reconciliation would take more than dinner. As she thought about it, a plan began to form. "Do you know if Josh has bought a Christmas tree?"

Clare looked puzzled. "I don't think so. He's been busy at the store. Why?"

"Because I'm going to show him what Christmas is all about. Then maybe he'll accept an apology."

"Are you planning a surprise attack?" Clare's eyes twinkled at the thought.

Lexa formulated exactly what she was going to do. "Not an attack. A homecoming."

"Do you need help?"

"No. But thanks for asking. This is something I have to do on my own." She stood up and smiled apologetically. "I won't have time for the tea."

Clare smiled. "Go do what you have to do so we can all have a happy Christmas."

Lexa stopped at a roadside tree stand and bought a three-foot evergreen. Stopping at a variety store, she bought ornaments and a star for the tree top. She also picked up a red and green elf's hat with a red tassel on the tip and strings of little bells. The next stop was the lingerie boutique, where she bought a bright red satin teddy, panties, and green net stockings. After she purchased eight helium foil balloons, half saying *I love you*, half printed with *Merry Christmas*, she shopped at a grocery store for all the ingredients she needed for supper.

Lexa drove to Josh's apartment, praying he wouldn't come home before the store closed. After peeling potatoes and scraping carrots, she placed the pot roast with the vegetables in the oven on low so she and Josh could eat whenever they felt like it. Talking could take a while. She caught her breath when she thought about the reunion that might follow. Quickly paring apples and mixing a crumb topping, she popped the apple crisp in the oven while she set up the Christmas tree on one end table. Attaching the helium balloons to the outside porch railing was difficult in the wind, but she managed.

Lexa changed into the teddy and stockings, and tied the bells around her ankles. She slipped on black spiked heels and added the hat at a jaunty angle on her head. Now all she needed was Josh.

Sitting in a corner of the sofa, she nervously paged through a magazine, plagued by doubts.

Lexa had jumped up and started down the hall to the bedroom when she heard someone coming up the back stairs. Oh, God. Josh.

She had scurried back to the living room when she heard more than one voice and realized Josh wasn't alone. She panicked. *What* was she going to do?

Lexa made it to the kitchen just as the men entered the living room. She plastered herself against the wall next to the refrigerator so she couldn't be seen and kept her feet still so she wouldn't jingle. She heard Josh say, "The cost estimates are what I expected, Tom. When do you think we can begin construction?"

Oh, Lord, Lexa thought. His contractor. There was no way she could make herself known. If he saw her, he'd think she was absolutely crazy, let alone what he'd think about Josh's taste in women. And if he left by the outside door, the balloons were flying . . . She swallowed hard and tried to remain calm so she could think her way out of this mess.

"We could begin by March first, weather permitting."

Lexa wondered why Josh didn't answer, but then she heard him say, "What the dickens?"

"What's wrong?" Tom Norman asked.

"This Christmas tree. It wasn't here when I left. I wonder if the employees thought I needed some cheering up."

"They come into your apartment?"

"They never have before."

"Do you cook?" Tom questioned.

"When I have to."

"It smells like someone's been cooking."

Lexa heard Josh's footsteps come near the kitchen. "I don't understand . . ." And then he saw her. Complete astonishment played over his face as Lexa put her finger to her lips to tell him not to give away her presence. He scrutinized her from head to toe, letting his eyes linger on her breasts, on the scant panties, on the lace stockings. She couldn't read the feelings behind his eyes as his face became expressionless.

Josh answered Tom. "Maybe someone has found some Christmas spirit and decided I shouldn't have to go to McDonald's on Christmas Eve. Would you like a beer?"

Lexa shook her head negatively to knock that idea out of Josh's head. She didn't want to be stuck against the wall any longer than necessary. If she moved, the bells would ring and give her away.

To her dismay, Tom answered, "Yeah. Sounds good. I'm not going back to the office."

Josh ignored the plea in Lexa's eyes as he opened the refrigerator, took out a bottle of beer, opened it, and found a glass. Without another look at her, he took it to the living room and gave it to Tom. "Are you doing anything special tonight?"

"We always go over to my mother-in-law's. The kids love it. They get presents tonight from all their relatives, and when they wake up tomorrow, they find the ones from Santa Claus. I guess I'm crazy, but I want to keep them kids as long as I can."

"You have four, right?"

"All boys. Man, can they make a ruckus. But that's the way kids are. Hey, what are you doin' tonight? Not spending it alone, are you?"

"I thought I was. But I suppose plans can change at the last minute."

"Have someone special in mind?"

"Maybe."

Lexa squirmed. He knew she could hear every word.

"Sometimes I envy guys like you. Bein' single, having variety. You get my drift."

If Josh didn't, Lexa did. She waited for Josh's reply.

"Yeah, there's something to be said for not being tied down."

Anger burned away Lexa's embarrassment. Okay. That did it. She was wearing more clothes than a woman on the beach in a bikini. If Mr. Norman didn't want to look, he didn't have to. She straightened herself on her high heels and, with bells ringing, walked into the living room.

"Well, Josh," she cooed. "Introduce me to your associate."

Tom Norman was staring at her as if she had dropped from the sky. He closed his mouth when Josh introduced them nonchalantly. "Tom Norman, meet Alexandra Kittredge."

Tom stuck out his hand, his eyes leveling at her breasts. "Howdy, ma'am. I didn't know anybody was here."

Lexa's voice was as sweet as a candy cane. "Oh, I just

dropped down Josh's chimney to see if he wanted some company tonight. You'd be surprised at the many people who need some Christmas cheer in their lives.''

Tom seemed to realize that this was more than surface conversation. After his eyes swept up Lexa's legs once more, he said to Josh, "I'd better be going. Thanks for the beer. Nice to meet you, Miss Kittredge.''

"You too," she returned brightly, wishing she could see his expression when he spied the balloons. But she couldn't. She did hear him say to Josh, "You have a Merry Christmas. You're a lucky devil.''

Lexa wasn't sure Josh agreed. When he closed the door and faced her, she was positive he didn't. There were tense lines around his mouth, and his eyes masked his emotions.

Her heart accelerated and she became defensive. "Why did you do that, Josh? Why did you try to make a fool out of me?"

His eyes were cold. *"Me?* Make a fool out of *you?"*

She snatched the hat from her head and threw it on the coffee table. "You could have gotten rid of him. You didn't have to offer him a beer and compare notes on the advantages of being single.''

"You didn't like the notes? Maybe we could have made them more graphic.''

Anger edged his words and ignited like sparks in her. "Stop it, Josh. I came here to . . ." She couldn't seem to find the right words.

"To what, Lexa? *For*what?" The anger in his eyes flashed. "Do you have any idea of the hell I've been through yesterday and today? Do you have any idea how many times I picked up that phone to call you and thought better of it?"

She crossed her arms across her breasts as if to protect herself. "You have every right to be angry.''

"You're damned right I do. You leave here without discussion, rejecting my proposal, saying I don't understand you." His hands clenched and unclenched at his sides while the nerve under his cheekbone twitched with turbulent emotions. "Dammit, Lexa, I think I understand you better than you understand yourself. To top it off, I walk in here with a business associate and you're dressed like that!" His eyes slid from her head to her toes. "How did you expect me to react?"

She blinked back tears. "I know it's kind of silly. But I wanted to do something special for you."

The lines in his forehead smoothed out, his jaw's frozen line softened. "I was scared, Lexa. I thought all kinds of things."

"What?" she asked softly, unfolding her arms.

"I thought you'd come back and tell me we were finished. I thought you'd come back and settle for me since you couldn't have a child. I prayed that you'd come back and tell me we still had a future."

"That's why I came back, Josh. Without your love, even having a child has lost its meaning. I want to be your wife, with or without children. You and me, together. That's what matters."

Josh's voice was heavy with emotion. "You know that you don't have to cook my meals, decorate a tree, or dress like an elf for me to love you? You don't have to *do* anything."

"Are you saying you still love me?"

His eyes were an intense blue, moist with feeling. "I'm saying I love you, I need you, and I want to spend the rest of my life with you."

Josh swept Lexa up in his arms and carried her to the bedroom. He laid her on the bed and stripped quickly.

His hands ran over her satin curves, spreading fire wherever he touched, then disrobing her quickly. His kisses were punishing in nature, demanding retribution, demanding a volatile response, demanding love he thought he might have lost.

Lexa held him with mounting passion as she caught his driving need, understood his untamed loving, and surrendered to him completely. His movements were frenzied, erratic, as his touches and strokes trailed flaming sensations.

Her fingers played wantonly wherever she could reach. Their bodies glistened as he plunged his tongue into her mouth, nipped at her shoulder, taunted, and lapped her breasts. Waves of delirious pleasure had her whole body quivering under his mouth and hands and he was quaking under hers.

He murmured, "I love you, Lexa." His voice was thick with need. "And I want you. God, how I want you."

Lexa's hands were trembling from her own desire and need. "I love you, too, Josh, and I want you. I want you so much."

Their lips sealed, their tongues danced in heated love play. Lexa arched her back, pressing into him, feeling his manhood urgent against her. His fingers found the eye of her desire—slick, satiny, ready for him. When she moaned and pressed against his hand, he petted and stroked until she was writhing against him and whispering his name in pleasure-ridden purrs.

Josh raised himself above her, his gaze a boundless ocean of love. "I want to love you for a lifetime. Can you accept my love? Can you accept everything I want to give you?"

He was totally vulnerable, allowing Lexa to see into his soul. The love that swept over her was so awesome, she trembled.

"Take me, Josh. Take me now," Lexa pleaded. She wanted him, all of him, filling her until they weren't two, but one, in perfect union.

He poised above her.

"What, Josh? What's wrong?"

"Nothing's wrong, sweetheart. Everything's right." When Lexa reached for him, a thick groan rose in Josh's throat. She took him in her hand and guided him between her thighs. He slowly let her know all of him, controlling his fierce desire to plunge to the center of her womanhood.

His voice was rough with the wonder of their fusing. "God, Lexa. You feel so good, so right."

She drew him deeper and deeper into herself. "I want to be part of you, Josh. For always."

Josh moved inside her, stroking precisely, pausing ever so slightly, lengthening each thrust, building a conflagration that was consuming them both. He kissed her fervently, trying to tell her what she meant to him, how much he loved her. He possessed her utterly, creating a new excitement that made Lexa claw his shoulders. He carried her further and further into pure sensation, yet closer and closer to himself. They called to each other, shaken with rippling sensations, and became as one in a blissful explosion of heat and light and love.

When Josh's heartbeat was beating more normally, he slid to his side but kept one leg thrown over hers possessively. He brushed her bangs away from her flushed face. "Was that as wonderful for you as it was for me?"

"Yes. Oh, yes," she confessed with amazement.

He caressed her cheek lovingly. "Lexa, I'm sorry about that business with Tom Norman. I never should have done that to you. I'm truly sorry."

She brushed her fingers over his sideburn. "I understand. You were angry."

"That's no excuse."

"I forgive you. Do you forgive me for the other night, the way I left?"

"Didn't I just prove I have?"

"I need to be sure."

He slid his thumb over her kiss-bruised lips. "I think I could forgive you anything as long as I know you love me."

"I do, Josh. I trust you too. Do you believe me?"

"Yes, I do." He broached the subject that had to be discussed. "How did it go with Dani?"

She snuggled farther into his shoulder. "Everything you said was right on the mark. I realized it on the drive home and after a talk with Dad. Dani and Rob want to make this work."

He tipped up her chin. "How do you feel?"

"I want Dani to be happy. I think my days of taking care of her are over. But I did want that baby, and part of me feels empty."

After a moment, Josh said, "I still do want children if that's what you want. We can seek out a specialist, adopt, whatever you want to do." Her eyes were so loving, so hopeful, so joy-filled, he had to kiss her.

A tear strayed down her cheek next to her nose. Josh swiped it away with his finger. "Are you happy?"

She nodded.

"Me, too." He rubbed his foot up and down her calf. "I do appreciate the tree, the supper, and the elf." He shook his head with exasperation. "I couldn't believe you were hiding in the kitchen in red satin with bells on your toes."

"Ankles," she corrected.

"After the shock of seeing you wore off, I didn't know whether I wanted to shake you until your teeth rattled or kiss you senseless."

"That Irish temper," she sighed theatrically. "How am I ever going to put up with it?"

He disentangled himself, rose from the bed, and rummaged in his dresser drawer. She thought she might have hurt his feelings, but he turned around with a wide smile and a tiny present in his hand. He dropped it on her stomach. "There are a few hours until Christmas, but I want you to open this now."

Her fingers shook as she tore off the gold bow and the green foil wrapping. She took the lid off the box and found a blue velvet one inside. She looked up at Josh.

He said, "Open it."

When she lifted the lid, she found a perfect heart-shaped diamond set in white gold. "Oh, Josh. It's beautiful."

He lay down beside her, took the ring from its velvet bed, and slipped it on her finger. "Will you promise to put up with my Irish temper?"

"Forever," she promised fervently.

"Forever," Josh pledged as his lips found hers and they sealed their vows.

Lexa slipped her hands under Josh's arms and hugged him tight. Together, they'd give thanks. Together, they'd raise a child someday, somehow. Together, they'd love.

Forever.